JUST HUMAN
by
Angel Hellyer

JUST HUMAN

The moral rights of Angel Hellyer to be identified as the author of this work have been asserted.

Copyright 2024
Hague Publishing
PO Box 451
Bassendean, Western AUSTRALIA 6934
Email: contact@haguepublishing.com
Web: www.haguepublishing.com

Identifiers:
eBook: ISBN 978-1-922984-06-7
softcover ISBN 978-1-922984-05-0

Cover and interior artwork by Obsidian Wax
Web: https://www.obsidianwax.art

DEDICATION

To Michael Beahan, for convincing me that I am creative.

30 MAY

I know writing in a diary is a bit pathetic, but the new school counsellor said everyone had to try it after everything that's happened. I think she's just overwhelmed by how many students want to see her and has no clue how to treat all the new problems everyone has (I mean, this stuff probably wasn't in her degree), so she's trying to fob us off with this whole "writing feelings down" thing. But I guess I'll give it a shot. And hey, you're my diary. It's not like you're going to tell anyone I'm doing this.

I should probably start at the beginning, when everything changed almost a year ago. You see, all those things like werewolves, vampires, druids and stuff used to be just make-believe. Stuff in books and shows that you dressed up as for Halloween, or that people believed back before there was science. Then they suddenly became real overnight. Or at least overnight where I am, and thankfully not on a full moon.

The worse part was that it happened to people who already had lives. Like, it wasn't that there were suddenly all these Creatures among us. No, it was <u>us</u>. About half the population suddenly became… something. Something other than human while still being themselves. It's complicated.

No one knows why it happened. Scientists say they have ruled out viruses or radiation. I mean, who thought it was radiation? This isn't a comic book. But they've also ruled out everything else, so I guess they're out of ideas.

The current theory most people are going with is that belief makes things real, and "young people" have been "engaging with the unreal" too much. Of course they blame us!

If that was the case, why didn't some god of pop music or books come around ages ago? I saw a video online the other day suggesting it's all atheists' fault for having stopped believing in religion and that the power of belief moved to the fantasy stuff instead. Another conspiracy theory. As if we didn't have enough of them BEFORE it all changed!

Anyway, I don't know why it happened. And I don't really care. I'm more focused on the fact that it's real, and I have to live with it.

What I do know is that my dad now has to be chained up on a full moon so he doesn't accidentally kill us all, like he did Fluffy Cat. I think he's still a bit messed up by that first time, but it's not like anyone knew before then. I have totally forgiven him, though it's hard not being able to have a pet anymore.

At least some knew what they were pretty early on. The elves suddenly had pointy ears, the pixies and valkyries had sprouted wings overnight, and when the vampires woke up and tried to go outside that morning, the flames and smoke sort of gave it away. Thankfully most were able to get out of the sun quickly, and that super healing fixed them right up. Though there was that hockey player who was out doing early practice on the school oval when the sun came up.

There is still a burnt patch of grass that everyone avoids. Weird that it hasn't grown over so many months later.

But it's not like they're using the oval much anyway. Even though school started back up after the panic of the first few months, people haven't been doing much sport. Not until they figure out what gives an "unfair advantage" and how to restructure the leagues. There are a lot of people arguing over that. I mean, can a selkie compete in swimming with humans? Does there need to be a vampire category in weightlifting? Would valkyries be allowed to be at boxing matches when there's the risk they could influence who wins?

Oh yeah, and there was that whole call for everyone who displayed non-human traits to be locked up. But with half the politicians now in that category and the others having loved ones who are, that wasn't ever going to happen.

Instead, they've cracked down on the human supremacy movements that were forming militias and are just trying to convince everyone to "get along". It's funny: racism and sexism seem to have reduced a lot since it happened. All it took was a worldwide calamity, and another group to think of as different.

According to the news, particularly the more conservative channels, some groups of non-human Creatures are banding together, thinking they're better than the other types (and, of course, better than humans). Ayan at school said there is some "vampires only" club starting a few towns over that serves blood from rare animals. And the valkyries at school have got their own little clique, although it's not an official club or anything. As if getting a say in who wins a fight is some awesome skill to have. Just don't get into a fight and it's fine. At least, that's my plan.

Either way, no matter what group we're talking about, us basic humans are at the bottom of the food chain.

Dad says maybe I'll still be something and that we don't know what will come out in time. So far, the only druids and muses we know of are adults or late teens, so there's a theory it's a puberty-related thing. By process of elimination, there's not much else left. There are no noticeable body changes. I'm no stronger or quicker than I used to be. And no matter how hard I try, I haven't been able to transform into anything.

It's so lame. Even my cousin Anna became a selkie. I mean, who had even heard of a selkie before? The scientists say there is a "statistically significant correlation" between the Creatures people turned into and the dominant cultures of the society, so the theory is all the Celtic immigrants made selkies happen here. But seriously, a seal? What good is being able to turn into a seal when we live inland?

Though it could be worse. The other day, I saw a video from China of this vampire guy that became so stiff he could only move by hopping.

Dad tells me that humans are interesting now, that we're needed to "continue the species" given we've got a much lower population than before, and we still don't know what happens when people of different species interbreed. But I know he's just saying that to make me feel better.

I mean, that's what dads are supposed to do. At least it's better than Mike's parents, who split up after the change because one couldn't handle the other being a dryad. Or maybe the dryad couldn't deal with his husband having been a lumberjack for twenty years. I guess that would be sort of weird. But now Mike gets to stay in a tree house every second week, which he says is cool but a bit limited in the cooking options given his dad is now terrified of fire.

And at least Mike is just human like me, so we can be basic and boring together.

Anyway, that's the state of the world. That's my life. It's all messed up, but at least school started back up so I can see people again. It was getting really rough those first few months, with Dad being too scared for me to go out, so I could only really contact people online or through text. Felt like back when COVID first happened.

My school has even started video streaming classes for the vampires, though they still complain about having to be awake during school hours. I mean, it's not like we're all going to adjust to nocturnal hours just for them!

Daisy Nguyen-Smith is the worst, of course. Because she thinks everything needs to be about her.

Vampires should just be glad we have digital photos and videos now, unlike the stuff that used silver from ages ago, where they couldn't check their makeup or have their picture captured.

Daisy's only response when someone said that to her was: "It's not like I touch silver, anyway. I'm all about the gold." Ugh.

She's probably annoyed that she's suddenly not getting everything her own way. Just because she used to be the most popular girl in school doesn't mean she still is. I swear, she must be layering on the fake tan trying to keep looking like she did. And the rumour is she's got herself some fancy coffin with rhinestones and satin lining.

No, the coffins aren't a real thing vampires need, but I wouldn't put it past Daisy to do it just to have the fanciest coffin around.

I can't really think of anything more to write just now, so I guess that will do. And it's not like it made me feel any better or anything.

But here it is. The diary of a normal human teenager. Pathetic, right?

2 JUNE

I had my school-mandated monthly counselling session today. I mean, I get why the school is doing it, but I don't need it. I'm fine, really. It's not like I need to drink blood, or randomly cry and screech. Those banshees are so annoying. Thank God there aren't many of them. The school counsellor, Ms. Hoxha, wanted me to share with her from this journal, but the idea made me feel really weird. I don't want her reading this. Not that I'm taking this seriously or anything; I just was supposed to write every day and have only written once so far. That's all.

Because I said no to her reading the diary, she wanted to talk about feelings and stuff. Even did the whole "How did that make you feel?" and "What is it you want?" stuff, head tilt and all. I thought that was just in the movies, but maybe they teach that to all the psych students.

And how am I supposed to know how it feels to have half the people you know suddenly become some sort of Creature? To have the world be totally different and no one knowing their place in it anymore? Even me, and I haven't changed.

At least I got out of that session early after all the incense Ms. Hoxha's constantly burning made me start coughing, and then I couldn't stop. I guess that's one benefit to being human, in a weird way: I still have my asthma. Some of the Creatures with super healing no longer have issues like that. Dad says I need to concentrate on the positives of being human, and I'm trying.

I don't know why she insists on burning incense all the time. I swear she'll set off the fire alarm someday with all that smoke. Maybe she's one of those new age groupies. According to the news, lots of humans have gotten into all the tarot cards and crystals and stuff to make themselves seem interesting to the critters.

Not that Dad likes me calling them that. He says it's "Creaturist". As if that's even a thing! How can I be the person being discriminatory when they get all the cool stuff? Everyone wants to be something new now. No one wants to hang out with the boring humans.

Anyway, that wasn't the most interesting thing to happen today. This afternoon, we all suddenly got called into an all-school assembly. Even the teachers didn't know what was happening, so we knew it had to be BIG. Mike was just happy we got out of Chemistry early. The teacher, Mr. Dane, thought enough of himself and too little of everyone else even before he became an elf.

So, we all filed into the hall. Not that there are that many of us. Small town, small school. But that made it even more interesting: everyone always knows the news immediately here, so surprises are rare.

On the stage, the principal was acting weird. I swear Mr. Rusico's chest was puffed out so far it matched his gut for once! He was wearing the suit he only wears for special events, like graduations and student-teacher nights. And up beside him on the stage was Adriana.

Oh, Adriana.

Oh yeah, I guess I should give the backstory. You're a book, after all, you don't know what happened.

So, Adriana, Mike and I were best friends growing up. She's a year older than us, but we all lived on the same street, so we used to hang out a lot as kids, and then through school.

I think the word is "inseparable". It was always the three of us, or at least two of us hanging out when the third couldn't convince their parents to let them come.

Then, one day, Adriana's parents caught me trying to kiss her. It was innocent, I swear! I mean, I was 13, and stuff was happening and I... I mean, she... it didn't mean anything!

But the Pereiras are super strict. They're all into this ultra-conservative evangelical church, one of those religions with people singing and talking in weird languages, which believes this whole Creatures thing is God's doing and found obscure Bible verses to try to justify it.

I did not know before this that there are vampires and werewolves in the Bible. There are even unicorns! I wish we'd gotten unicorns when the change happened, but for some reason it only affected humans, as far as we know so far.

But yeah, her parents freaked. That was the last time we were allowed to hang out.

Adriana's not even allowed to talk to me at school. She crosses the hallway when I'm near, just in case her parents see us near each other, though she at least sometimes gives me a guilty look for it.

And today, her parents were also right there, beaming alongside Mr. Rusico. Adriana had that half-smile she gets when she's super uncomfortable and just wishes the ground would open and swallow her whole.

Her hands were clutched so tight in front of her pleated tartan skirt that I could see the knuckles whitening. Why did her parents insist she wears what looked like a uniform, anyway? We weren't one of those fancy schools where everyone had to dress alike, and Adriana hates how those knee-high socks keep falling down when she walks, no matter how many elastics she uses.

"You OK?" Mike had whispered to me.

He knew the whole thing, of course. He'd been cut off at the same time, even though he'd done nothing wrong. But the Pereira's had decided that Adriana needed "better influences" in her life than us. Which, of course, meant no socialising with anyone at school.

I felt terrible about that, but Mike never blamed me for destroying our group. He is great like that. The best friend I could hope for. And it's just been us two since then.

"Sure," I replied. "Course." I was fine. Totally.

Thankfully we all had to sit down and be quiet right after that. Except for the five people on stage: Mr. Rusico, the Pereiras, and an elf standing to the side of the stage looking like a Secret Service agent from an action movie, crew cut and all, with a coiled cord going into one pointy ear.

The principal took his time, relishing the drama and expectation. He droned on for a while about how wonderful the school was, how this was the proudest moment in his teaching career, building up the suspense with some words that meant nothing. He literally had someone from the school band do a drumroll.

Then he announced it: Adriana had been discovered to be a muse.

I DID NOT cry. Not at all.

Nope.

But…

She deserves it. So much.

Muses are one of the most sought-after Creatures there are. Even junior ones, after they do some initial training with some ritual or something (they're super secretive about it), get hundreds of offers from schools wanting to inspire their students to get better grades. And those who are strongly talented are poached by major corporations in seconds.

I saw an article recently saying that the rates of new inventions being patented rose nearly 75 percent in the last six months, even though businesses were in freefall during the panic after the change. It said they think that's almost all from the influence of the muses.

Adriana is set for life. It's like the new version of winning the year's biggest lottery.

Not that she'd be getting that life right now. Her parents said they wanted her to stay in school, to finish her senior year before moving for her muse training. That was just like them, to stand in the way of her becoming what she was meant to be because they want her to follow the "right" path.

At one point, I swear Adriana caught my eye. I tried to smile. I mean, it was so great for her! She was going to make it, to get out of this town and make something of herself. She would probably travel the world and have so many adventures. I am happy for her. Really.

She looked away too quickly for me to tell if she'd seen.

Mr. Rusico let us all go home early after that. To "celebrate the greatness Adriana was bringing to our little town" by being a muse, even one who couldn't use her abilities yet.

Muses are a bit weird like that. They've got to spend some time with other muses before their powers fully materialise. No one knows why yet, given it was only discovered about six months ago when a group of people who thought they were just human were hanging out, and suddenly weird things started happening. Like much of what's happening now, we just don't know how it all works.

But, somehow, those whose powers have manifested know other muses instantly, so they send people around to schools for testing. Not obviously, of course. No assembly or class for it. Just like everything else the muses do, it's done in secret.

I understand that, though; with how in demand they are, there have been reports of muses being coerced into "helping" people. And that elf on stage turned out to be a security guard sent by the local Chapter of Muses to keep Adriana safe. They would be "accompanying" her at all times.

Adriana will hate that. She likes having quiet time to herself. Sitting in the backyard alone, listening to music, or going for a bushwalk to just lie down and read in the sun, even though it gives her freckles.

After we left the auditorium, Mike wanted to head out to the park to hang out and see if he could get a nice acorn to give his dad. The most common tree for Dryads is an oak, so acorns are special and stuff, and Mike had heard of a stash of acorns from last year that some animal must have made and forgotten about.

I told him that I couldn't go out with him though, that my father needed me because it's a full moon. He always wants me home well before he gets ready to transform so he knows I'm safely in my room, away from the cage. And, sometimes, he's a bit emotional before he shifts and needs some support.

Sure, he's got the werewolf support group that helps keep an eye on him through the night. And, of course, that includes giving me a "babysitter". As if I need one at my age?

Anyway, that's why I decided to come home and not spend time with Mike in the park. To look after Dad.

So, I should go do that. Bye for now.

3 JUNE

Adriana. That was all ANYONE could talk about at school today.

I mean, yeah, I get it. It's great that she's a muse and she'll get out of this place and be all successful. No one deserves that more than Adriana, and I really am so happy for her.

But that's ALL they care about. To the point that I almost wanted someone to talk about the latest episode of whatever crappy teen romance show is popular now, or some stupid thing a sports star did lately.

When I walked in this morning, this huge group of people was mobbing Adriana. I didn't know that to begin with, though.

It took me ages to see through the crowd to find out what was going on. To see Adriana there in her pressed white blouse and perky blond ponytail, standing in the middle, shadowed by her bodyguard in black. Shoulders hunched, staring at the ground. She was so uncomfortable. I just wanted to save her.

I couldn't, of course. I mean, it would be social suicide to have a nobody like me try to save her. I wouldn't do that after she'd finally gotten her ticket out of the nobody club.

Daisy even arranged to have a video she'd made for Adriana shown on the school TV screens before classes started. There were love heart emoji and this awful pop tune. Probably something her dad wrote.

He thinks he's still some music star when he was only ever B-grade anyway, and that was decades ago. The only way people under thirty even knew he was ever sort of famous was from looking back at retro cassette tapes.

Daisy droned on with some crap about how she'd always known Adriana was special. Gross. Daisy used to tease Adriana every chance she got!

I bet she's just upset her move from being the most popular girl in school has been confirmed. It was bad enough that she couldn't be here in person during the day to reign as the school queen, but now we have a muse.

Even the weird kids tried to get some of Adriana's time. I saw some of the goths go over, before the popular kids pushed them out of the way. That didn't seem like a smart move to me, with all the buckles and spikes and stuff some of them were wearing, but the goths just walked away with a few raised middle fingers.

And even the teachers weren't immune. They kept going on and on about it in class, even though Adriana isn't even in our year! I almost enjoyed Chemistry for once, because Mr. Dane was the one teacher who didn't spend at least ten minutes talking about it. He did spend that long finding ways to talk about how great he is and how we all failed him on our last test, but that's normal for Mr. Dane.

Mike seemed really cut by it, though. Chemistry just isn't his thing, and I wish he could transfer out. But he's so obsessed with doing well in school to help his dads feel better about the separation, and he doesn't want them to think he isn't trying. I tried to tutor him, and he at least got a pass this time, but it's hard to see him struggling.

And I swear Mr. Dane picks on Mike. I thought it might be a racist thing, but he doesn't do it to other black kids in the class. He once even told Mike that his ADHD was "not an excuse" for poor grades and refuses to make any adjustments to make things easier for Mike.

To make things worse, Mr. Dane seems to love me just because my sibling, Leigh, did really well in Chemistry and is off studying it at uni. It's weird because Leigh also has ADHD, and I am OK at Chemistry, but it's not like I get A's or anything. But he's always nice to me (or at least as nice as he ever gets) and cruel to Mike.

After Chemistry was lunch, which was about as awful as the morning before school had been.

We had lunch at the same time as Adriana and the crowd was around her again. Adriana usually eats her lunch in the library, but it's closed for a few days for renovations, so she was stuck being around people. I can't imagine how uncomfortable she was.

Ayan, the drama nerd, did this weird performance thing for Adriana. Some sonnet from Shakespeare, supposedly. I don't know; it was full of words like "thou" and "dost" and made no sense to me.

Adriana's gorgeous blue eyes grew so wide I thought she might faint. Though she does look cute when she blushes like that. It starts in her cheeks, travels up her face and then down her neck. Like, you can tell how embarrassed she is by how low it goes. Not that her parents allow her to wear anything low-cut anymore. It wouldn't be "proper" to show that much skin now that she's a "young lady".

When the stupid monologue ended, Ayan knelt on one knee and presented a rose to Adriana. I swear her face was nearly as red as that flower.

How could no one else see that she didn't want this attention? That she just wanted to go on as a normal person rather than the centre of the school's social circle?

I'm glad Mike had been with me. If not, I don't know if I could have stopped myself from going over. And at least I could help him when I couldn't help Adriana, so I concentrated on that.

He had his monthly counselling session coming up after lunch and felt weird about it. He'd gone to counselling outside of school when everything happened and his dads split, but he'd hated it. The shrink they'd sent him to, the only one in our town, had become a druid and gotten all about natural therapies. When he'd discovered Mike was on meds for his ADHD, he'd tried to persuade Mike's dads to abandon it in favour of some herbal fix, saying that the meds were "unnatural" and bad for him.

Mike's dads reported the psych to some professional board and he was banned from practising, but the whole experience had given Mike a really bad view of psychs. His dads had tried to get him into one in the next town over, but he'd refused.

So I tried to ignore Adriana's plight and focused on helping Mike. That's what a friend does, right? I mean, I could help Mike where I couldn't help Adriana. And really, wasn't the attention Adriana was getting what most teenagers want in school? She'd need to get used to it, anyway. Once she was a full muse, she'd have people trailing her every watery step.

I still don't get why muses have the dripping footstep thing. I remember hearing something about them being linked to water nymphs, but Adriana didn't resemble any of those paintings I'd seen of Greek nymphs. Women coming out of lakes covered in nothing but a gauzy fabric that somehow floated in the breeze even though it must have been wet.

I stopped myself from going down that thought path at school, and kept chatting with Mike. By the time lunch was over, he seemed a bit cheerier but still not looking forward to the counsellor session.

I didn't see him for the rest of the day since we had no classes together. I texted him to see how he's feeling, and I'm sure he'll respond soon.

Until then, I have way too much homework to do. I should do that instead of writing in this diary. Not that I enjoy this, of course. I still think it's stupid. But maybe it will take a bit longer to do anything to help, so I guess I'll try for a few more days.

7 JUNE

Mr. Dane is dead!

Like, really, actually, deceased. Heartbeat flatlined, and not in a "became a vampire" kind of way.

Chemistry class started out normal. We're doing Chemistry of Ecology this term, and Mr. Dane had us doing this experiment about how limestone forms and dissolves and stuff. I was working with Mike and we got our piece of limestone and put it onto a piece of metal gauze. Mike set up the Bunsen burner, opened the gas valve and got the flame going nice and hot, mainly blue.

Then Megan started speaking up. She used to be called Jane, but she changed her name after some comic book character that her mum loves when she became a pixie.

Oh, that reminds me that I heard some old commentator guy saying the other day that calling them pixies is "woke" and only done by "snowflakes". I mean, sure, they're technically more like fairies from myths, but that word has been used to hurt people, so we use "pixies" instead. Is it really that big a deal to just use a different word that doesn't hurt people? I don't understand some people.

Anyway, Megan had already been VERY vocal about disability rights and accessibility and stuff before the change, and then she added pixie and general Creature rights to her campaigning. And Mr. Dane was one of her favourite targets, since he never cared about anyone but himself.

I don't remember the exact words, but she said something like: "Mr. Dane, I have already informed the school that the use of Bunsen burners is a discriminatory practice. As you are well aware, because I have told you repeatedly, they are made of metals that are harmful to pixies." I swear, her voice just kept getting louder and louder as she said it, until she was nearly screaming.

Mr. Dane didn't seem phased by her outburst. He raised an eyebrow, which somehow seemed even more condescending now that he has had the pointed elf ears. Which, of course, he showed off as much as possible, even getting a new haircut after the change to ensure everyone knew he was an elf.

His response had been less than sympathetic. Even if I remembered the words, I'm sure I couldn't write them as arrogant and patronising as they were. It was along the lines of: if the school had enough money to refurbish the chemistry labs to make them pixie-accessible, they would spend that money to get a trained muse instead to give Megan the inspiration to wear gloves.

Megan DID NOT take that well. I don't blame her, but I don't think I've ever seen a person go quite so red with rage. Like, it was something out of an anime.

She said some things that included words I know Dad would not approve of me using, and some others I'd never heard before. Her wings beat so fast that she rose from the ground while yelling. It was only a threat of being sent to the principal ("for obscene language") that made Megan sit down, but her face didn't go back to normal and she started typing rapidly, probably taking notes for a formal complaint.

About then, Mike got my attention. He'd been heating the limestone as we'd been told to, and it had started glowing slightly. He whispered to me, concerned that he'd done something wrong, but was obviously not quiet enough.

From the bench behind us, Ayan broke the awkward silence in the classroom to tell Mike (and, given it was Ayan, loud enough to "project" through the whole classroom) that the glowing was "limelight". He helpfully informed us about how it used to be used in theatres, which is where we get the saying about being "in the limelight" from.

I could tell Mike didn't appreciate the limelight of the whole room coming onto him in the form of Mr. Dane loudly pronouncing that, for once, Mike had done the right thing. Then he lowered the lights in the room to make it easier to see the glow from the rocks.

I gave Mike a reassuring look but wished I could have done more. It wasn't fair for him to be singled out like that.

The experiment continued. We added some water and took some measurements, then tested the pH. Then it was time to note down the chemical reactions. I helped Mike with that bit and talked him through what I was doing. I mean, I'm not great at Chemistry, but the basic reaction stuff makes sense to me, which it just doesn't to Mike.

I know that doesn't make me any smarter than Mike, but I think he thinks it does, which I hate.

Anyway, I was in the middle of explaining why it had become more alkaline when Mr. Dane decided there hadn't been enough drama in the class and pulled Megan up for not completing her experiment because she'd been too busy typing.

He started by saying, "Jane, oh, I mean Megan, if you don't participate in this experiment, I will have to deduct points from your grade. And you know you're barely passing as it is."

Wrong on SO MANY levels! First, such obvious deadnaming to just be awful. Then talking about her grades in front of everyone? Megan is super smart, but everyone knows Dane "adjusts" scores based on how much he likes people.

Megan must have pulled herself together a bit by this point and decided to go for smugness instead of anger, even with such obvious goading. I swear, no lie, that her exact words were, "Oh, don't worry, Mr. Dane. My grades won't be your concern for much longer."

Mr. Dane opened his mouth to respond. Then he started clutching at his chest and collapsed to the floor.

I… I just sat there. I didn't know what to do. There was yelling and screaming, and some people went to check on him, but I just sat there. I wanted to move, to help, but I couldn't. It was like I was paralysed. I just watched, as the hand grasping his chest went limp and flopped to the floor.

"Sudden cardiac arrest," the paramedics supposed. I don't remember when they got there, but I was outside the room by that point and overheard them as they wheeled away a body-shaped lump covered by a white sheet.

I don't even remember how I got outside, but I must have somehow. The next thing I knew, I was leaning against the lockers in the hallway, with Mike beside me.

Mr. Rusico and Ms. Hoxha were there. Had they been speaking to us? There was this weird buzzing sound that made it hard to understand anything, and my vision seemed blurry on the edges.

Eventually, I turned to Mike, but he seemed even more shocked than me. I saw tear marks down his cheeks and his eyes were wide open, but he seemed to be staring at nothing.

A little part of me wondered if Mike was glad Mr. Dane had died. I know they say it's wrong to speak ill of the dead, but am I awful for sort of thinking he deserved it? He'd been so cruel to Mike. Maybe I was a little glad? I hoped I wasn't.

I reached out a hand and grabbed Mike's. His face didn't change, but he squeezed my hand back.

Our parents showed up not long after. The school must have called them. Mike's dads both arrived around the same time and, for once, had something to bond over rather than fight as they cared for their son.

My dad was only a minute behind them. I was a little surprised the bank let him leave, even for this. He's always being forced to work ridiculous hours. I mean, I know banks are trying to recover after the financial crash that happened with the change, but he works so many late nights (except for on full moons, of course), and he's so tired when he gets home. I wish they'd cut him some slack.

We all had to wait until the police came and took all our names and addresses. Dad wanted to talk, but I didn't. I just stood there, watching Mike as he sat down, head bowed, one of his dads on either side and looking over him at each other in worry.

When we were eventually allowed to leave the school, the red and blue lights of the cop cars outside kept flashing and flashing, making everything seem like we were in a movie.

Walking was weird. Like, I knew I was putting a foot forward, then another, but I couldn't really feel it. My brain felt separate from my body, like my body was on autopilot or something.

As Dad started the car and pulled out of the car park, I saw two stocky police officers walking to a cop car, one on either side of Megan. Her hands were behind her back, which meant she had to lean on one of the cops while the other carried her walking cane. Couldn't they at least have let her walk to the car before cuffing her? That seemed really cruel, especially with how the cuffs would set off her arthritis.

For once, Megan didn't seem to have a word to say. She stared blankly ahead, her face pale and bleak.

For a moment, I thought she had looked my way. It was just a moment, but her bright green pixie eyes seemed weirdly empty. Then she bowed her head as one cop not-so-gently guided her into the back of the police car.

Dad drove around a corner, so I couldn't see any more after that. He tried to talk with me on the way home, but it seems I had nothing to say either.

I hope Megan is OK. I really do.

7 JUNE . . . AGAIN

Ugh, Dad is being all weird. I mean, yeah, I'm freaked out by what happened today, but he keeps trying to get me to talk. I mean, what is there to say?

I saw my teacher die, right in front of me. And I didn't do anything about it. And people think my classmate is somehow responsible.

The school forum online is full of photos people took of Megan getting arrested. Then there were some of her mother pleading with the police, but them ignoring her as they marched Megan out. The people on the forum kept saying she killed Mr. Dane, calling her awful names and making out as if he was some sort of saint.

Maybe I should be more upset about it all. But once you've lived through half the world becoming critters and all the messed up stuff that came with that, it just feels like one more death isn't that big a deal. Is that strange? Am I wrong to think that?

I mean, the weeks after the change were filled with stories of death. Werewolves rampaging on their first transition. Vampires unable to control their hunger. Valkyrie going into murderous rages when they got upset.

The sound of banshees screaming was almost as common in those days as an emergency vehicle siren, and they were often about the same things.

So the death of one teacher just doesn't seem as big a deal as it would have beforehand. Especially someone as cruel as Mr. Dane.

Of course, I didn't tell Dad that. I just told him I was OK, but he didn't believe me. So, after the most awkward dinner we've ever had – even worse than the one where he tried to apologise about the cat, or after everything went down with Adriana and her parents had called to chew him out – I said I was tired and going to get some sleep.

I don't like lying to Dad. He is a good parent overall. I know he wants to help, but he can't. He just doesn't get what it's like for me, which isn't his fault.

Strangely, I am really tired suddenly, after all this writing. Maybe I should get some sleep.

8 JUNE

It was so weird at school today. Instead of our usual first classes, they called everyone in my Chemistry class into the hall. They made us all sit down the front, and we only took up the first few rows. I saved a seat next to me for Mike, who rushed in just as the principal started talking.

Mr. Rusico looked even more rumpled than usual, the opposite of the last assembly I'd seen him at. Instead of his usual way of walking around with his chest out proud, today his shoulders were curled in, and he looked even older. The four cops standing at the side of the stage, still and tall in their pressed uniforms with hands behind their backs, almost seemed like they were mocking the principal by contrast.

He said some stuff about how great Mr. Dane had been and how it was a tragedy, and I tried not to scoff at it. I looked at Mike to let him know how dumb I thought that was, but he had just sat there, head down as if he was actually upset.

Maybe he was. Maybe I should be? Was it wrong that I wasn't?

Anyway, after that, we were taken one by one for an interview with the police. I was one of the first called in and sat opposite a desk from an older guy with more grey than brown hair and a build that my dad would tell me was politely called "sturdy".

Next to him was a skinny officer who looked like they'd barely hit twenty and only spoke up when the older guy invited them to. The counsellor was also there, supposedly to protect the interests of us kids, but she never said anything in my interview. The biggest reaction she made was when a car alarm went off outside, and she nearly jumped from her seat in fright.

I guess Mr. Dane's death had been a bigger deal for the other school staff than for me.

The older cop asked a lot of questions about Megan, though he called her Jane and I kept having to correct him.

"Did she have a history of violence?"

"Did she have any opportunity to poison Mr. Dane?"

"Did I see her make any motions toward him?"

"Was there any evidence she could do magic?"

I mean, magic? Really? After all we've been through, everyone knows pixies don't have "magic" other than their strange ability to fly. They're just really annoying for some reason. Last I heard, that wasn't a crime, or my cousin Anna would have been in jail long ago.

The cops seemed to just assume Megan was guilty, even though there was no way she could have done it, other than maybe irritating Mr. Dane into a heart attack. I tried to say that, but the older one made some comment about how "You can never tell with these critters. Could have lots of powers they haven't told us about."

Those cops were both humans. The police force in my state passed a requirement early on to include what officers were on their badges, supposedly to help prevent misuse of supernatural force. There was a big fuss about it from those who'd changed, saying it was an invasion of privacy, but the people in charge were humans after the previous police chief decided to step down.

He'd become a banshee, and the screaming when death was near was freaking out all the cops. One younger officer had gotten so scared she'd shot an innocent person thinking they were about to kill someone. It turned out that was the imminent death, which is a weird thought puzzle I decided not to explore.

After that, a human police chief was brought in at the state level and, though there wasn't a formal ruling or anything, all the non-human local chiefs got "reassigned".

Come to think of it, all the cops I saw at the school today were human. Weird, given there were four of them. Statistically, I would have expected at least one to be a Creature.

Anyway, the interview didn't take long since I had nothing to say that they wanted to hear. I was out of there before my second class of the day. That was Maths, which made me almost wish the cops had taken longer. Except that I swear one of them was a smoker because I kept smelling smoke and it made my chest start to tighten up in the way it does just before I need my asthma puffer, and even Maths isn't bad enough for an asthma attack.

Mike had just gotten out of his interview at the morning break, and he seemed really spooked by it. Again, I wondered if maybe I should be too. I mean, someone had died in front of me. Then again, it could have just been that Mike was black. The cops certainly didn't have the best reputation for working with black kids.

Mike didn't have much to say during the break, or over lunch either, and he didn't want to walk home together.

I had wanted to say something to cheer him up, but didn't know what. I mean, how do you console a friend about this sort of thing? Especially if you don't know what's wrong.

Now that I write this down, I am really worried about Mike. What if the cops said or did something really awful and he's hurting? I'd like to think he would tell me about it, but I also know I don't understand what it's like for him. I can try to, but I'm not black so I'll never really get it.

But what can I do? I tried to check if he was OK, and he kept saying he was, even though he obviously wasn't. I mean, I've known Mike for as long as I can remember. I can read his moods and he knows it. But how do I help if he doesn't want to talk about it?

Maybe I should talk to one of his dads and get them to check on him? His Black dad would understand much better than me if it was something the cops did.

Yeah, I might do that right now.

9 JUNE

Mike is REALLY angry at me for talking to his dad. As in, he sent me an extra-long message this morning before school with lots of all caps that included the word "betrayed" multiple times.

I sent him lots of messages saying I was sorry, but he left them on read. I even tried calling him, which he knows I would only do about something important, and he sent me to message bank after two rings!

His text wasn't fully clear, but it sounds like his dads had a long talk with him last night after I talked with his druid dad. His lumberjack dad is going to take time off work to be home more, and his dads agreed not to have him move between the two homes for a bit, so he doesn't get to sleep in the tree house anymore.

And they're making him go to the school counsellor more, which he seemed super annoyed about. I mean, I don't like Ms. Hoxha much myself, but she's not that bad. You just give her some platitudes, say you're cool with everything, and she lets you go.

But I know it's not that easy for Mike.

How was I supposed to know all of that would happen? I just sent Mr. Musa a text saying I was worried about Mike, and then he called me back and spoke to me about it, and I told him how Mike had been at school. I don't think I made anything out to be worse than it was.

And maybe it's a good thing. I mean, Mike's dads are both nice, even Mike thinks so, and this has them talking again. And Mike could probably use some extra support with everything.

I tried to tell him that this morning when I saw him in the hallway, after he didn't meet me in our usual spot. But he just glared at me and literally walked away without a word, like something from some teen drama.

I've never seen Mike like that. Like, never. And I've known him as long as I can remember.

I want to help Mike. I really do! But he won't let me in.

He didn't talk to me all day. I ended up having lunch alone. And, of course, this was a day I had lunch at the same time as Adriana and had to watch everyone fawning over her. Still.

Well, except for Daisy. She seems to have gotten over her attempts to buy Adriana's attention to help her own status and moved on to pretending Adriana doesn't exist and definitely hasn't taken her top spot in the school popularity contest. I think Adriana is probably glad about that. She would have hated dealing with someone as vapid as Daisy.

Yeah, see Mrs. Liu, sometimes I do pay attention in English class and learn new words!

The only time anyone spoke to me at lunch was when they wanted to know more about how Mr. Dane died. Some of the emo kids came by asking whether I'd seen "the moment that his life was extinguished" and what his eyes were like. Gross.

Then Tanya asked if I'd seen the magic Megan had used and wouldn't believe me when I said there hadn't been any. She was just like the cops, assuming Megan had done it. I've heard that her mum is all into anti-Creature conspiracy theories about how this is part of a plot for world domination from some ancient underground organisation. If it is, they're doing a lousy job of it.

Ayan thought it was hilarious to overact that "To be or not to be" monologue from Hamlet, which is all about dying, then he clutched his chest and fell to the ground. That wasn't cool. I mean, he was there! He saw it. Sure, Mr. Dane was awful, but that's just gross.

I seemed to be one of the few people to think so, though. Everyone else was laughing, even those who usually roll their eyes at Ayan.

Well, except for Adriana. I swear I caught her eye for a moment, and she was just as disgusted as I was. But then she looked away and pretended there was something really interesting in her salad sandwich. On rye and sliced along the diagonal; the same lunch her mother always makes.

I was almost glad when the bell rang and it was time to go back to class. Especially because it was time for Modern History, and that's a class I have with Mike. We always sit together and have a game where we tally the number of times we study how people in power do stupid things because of their egos. At the end of the year, we're going to buy that many chocolate bars to keep us going through the holidays. I think we've already got enough to have one each day for the entire break, and we're only a few weeks in.

Well, that's if Mike forgives me before then. He came in just before the final bell and sat at an empty table at the back of the classroom. I tried to catch his eye as he walked past me, but he didn't look my way at all.

And, like, he was totally obvious about it, to the point that everyone looked at him walk right past me to that seat. Then looked right at me.

I thought I might die.

Maybe I shouldn't write that after everything that's happened.

I think the class was about something stupid done by Napoleon while trying to invade Russia. It sounded like something Mike and I would have had good laughs at, but I didn't pay much attention. Being alone at the desk felt weird when Mike was only metres away.

And although I tried to wait for him after class, Mike deliberately went the other direction, even though I know his class wasn't that way.

I sent him another message apologising, saying I was only trying to help.

It's still sitting unread.

I guess I should go to bed then. Homework is done, and I'd usually be gaming online with Mike tonight. But he hasn't logged in. So yeah, I guess bed it is.

10 JUNE

Mike still hasn't forgiven me. Still doing the silent treatment and not responding to my texts. Not even the funny memes, and I spent hours finding ones he'd love!

I've been thinking of messaging his dad again, but that will probably only make things worse.

I don't know what to do.

I know Dad would say to wait and give him time, but Mike's really my only friend. Pathetic, I know. But we've been friends for so long, and he understands what it's like being a human when we were both already outcasts before the change.

It's not like I can easily find other people like that. I mean, we don't have a human pride club at school. Technically, we are half the population, so not a minority, so people say we don't need a club, but I'm not so sure. We're the ones who got left behind.

So, let me think… what else happened today?

Oh, we got a new Chemistry teacher. Just a substitute for now, but they seem pretty cool. At least they're trying to make things more interesting in the class. We did an experiment today with sodium, and they were joking about how they used to get balls of sodium and hit them off a boat with a golf club into a river to watch them explode when they hit the water. And then, of course, warned us NEVER to do it.

Where would I buy sodium from anyway? It's not like it's on eBay or Amazon. I checked.

They were also super helpful about the experiment and actually explained it, rather than just making us muddle along the steps in the textbook like Mr. Dane did. I thought it was almost fun.

I say "I", because I was alone in the class. And not because Mike sat elsewhere this time. He wasn't in the class and I don't know why.

I sent him another message, letting him know what he missed, but he didn't reply to that either. I'm really getting worried about him.

Ugh, I have to stop thinking about him. There's nothing I can do!

Anyway, there were a couple of other interesting things today.

The first was Daisy's latest attempt to be relevant. While she was on video at lunch (something the school set up with all the vampires so they could still catch up with their classmates as a "Vampire inclusion program"), she started drinking from a bottle shaped like a curvy woman, and everyone around me started talking about it. They kept saying this name I don't know but, from what I could put together, it sounded like it was some social media influencer's new brand of blood that hasn't even been released yet.

I mean, I personally think it's poor taste (pun intended) to drink blood from a bottle shaped like a person. Drinking human blood was outlawed within weeks of the change, as soon as they figured out that animal blood and synthetic blood are good enough for vampires, and started organising production lines. There are still rumours of vampire fanatics who offer themselves for feeding, but I don't know if that's true or just from some silly book from before the change. I mean, it's gross, right? Isn't the general point of blood to remain on the inside?

Anyway, Daisy pretended not to notice the fuss over her lunch, though she made lots of lip-smacking motions and happy sounds each time she drank. It was almost as pathetic as how impressed everyone seemed.

Daisy has suggested a few times that she might be an actress one day, but she's got a LOT to learn based on that performance. I mean, even Ayan's a better actor than Daisy, and he's over the top even compared to the Shakespearean plays I've been forced to watch for English class.

Anyway, that's basically all people talked about while I sat alone at lunch, eating my vegan sausage, mashed potatoes and peas. The cafeteria has gone full vegan since the change so that they don't offend druids or tempt werewolves. The dryads still sometimes complain about specific species of plants, saying they're close to sentient, but the school says there's only so much they can do.

I tried to force lunch down quickly so I could head outside and away from the stupidity. But, of course, it started storming just as I finished. It's like the world wants me to be miserable.

Or maybe someone at school is a yeti and thought it would be funny. I read a rumour about yetis being able to bring on poor weather to make themselves more comfortable. Not that any scientists have yet confirmed that anyone has turned into a yeti, but who knows what's out there?

Anyway, I just sat for a while and read the latest on this Creature-watcher website that's gotten really popular, then went to English.

Classes were cut short today, with the last session replaced by a memorial thing for Mr. Dane. I was glad, in a way: that class was PE and, with the weather outside, we would have probably done something stupid like dodgeball. How do schools get away with something so aggressive and awful just by calling it sport?

Anyway, it was a morbid thing. Mr. Rusico was wearing a black suit and tie, which isn't his style and was a bit tight across his stomach. Must be his funeral suit. I guess his special occasion suit is only for happy occasions.

He kept going on about how wonderful Mr. Dane was. How he will be missed.

What a liar! I remember overhearing Mrs. Lui talking to another teacher about how awful Mr. Dane was one afternoon when I had to come back because I'd forgotten a book. I think her exact words were, "I envy everyone who has never met him."

The other teacher responded, "The only reason he believes in the heliocentric model is that he thinks the sun shines out of his ass." I had to look that one up before realising how funny it was.

This memorial thing was basically an hour of stupidity as teacher after teacher spoke empty words about Mr. Dane. I noticed most of them were men, though, and particularly white men. Says a lot.

I suffered through it, checking my phone whenever I thought no one was watching.

Still no Mike. Still no message.

Dad picked me up because of the weather, which was good but also meant I had to deal with him asking all those questions about how I'm doing, checking that I'm OK, and wondering if he needs to make an appointment with a therapist.

That's his solution to everything. When I was upset that Leigh moved out for university, he asked if I wanted to see a therapist. When the world changed, he kept pushing me to see one. And now again. Surely the school counsellor is enough!

I mean, I don't have anything against psychology. I just don't need it.

I guess I should be happy that he cares so much, but I'm seriously fine. I mean, I miss Leigh more than I'm freaked about the change or Mr. Dane's death, and we still keep in touch. And I was used to being boring before the change, and I'm still boring.

Yeah, someone died in front of me. And that's freaky and gross and stuff. But I think I'm used to freaky and gross now. That's just what life is now.

Anyway, Dad dropped me off and then had to go back into the office. Something about an acquisition case where the books needed to be perfect before the deal.

The storm was still wild. Rattling windows and all that stuff they say in horror books. The news said it was unexpected, hadn't shown up on radar until only moments before the rain started. They were already reporting lots of traffic accidents, and I got a bit worried about Dad driving back to work. I sent him a text asking him to let me know he got there OK, but it didn't send because of a network outage from the storm.

OK, so I got a bit stressed. Not bad, but bad enough that I couldn't concentrate on my homework. So I started looking up more about yetis on Creature forums.

The storm ended about an hour after I got home.

Weirdly, I wish it hadn't. Being home alone is always so quiet. The noise of the storm had hidden that for a bit. And I still hadn't heard from Dad.

Anyway, I played some games and now I'm writing in this stupid journal. And still waiting for both Dad and Mike to message me back. Even just tag me in a meme or something, no matter how pathetic it would be if it was from Dad.

I really hope they're OK.

What am I even going to do this weekend without Mike? I mean, a few new shows have been released, but that's about it. Dad will probably be working all weekend with this acquisition thing, and no new games look interesting.

I should probably work on my history assignment, but let's be real. I'd rather watch crappy 90s sitcoms all weekend, and I hate them. Anyway, it's not due for weeks.

Just got a text from Dad! He's fine. Just finishing up a few things at work, and then he'll be home.

I'm actually feeling really relieved. Maybe everything with Mr. Dane and Mike is getting to me more than I realised. But I'm sure I'll be fine. It's just been a lot in a short time.

OK, I really should do my homework for tomorrow. No more excuses.

Ugh. Why is there always more homework?

15 JUNE

Mike FINALLY started talking to me again!! Or at least he texted me this afternoon saying he is willing to talk, but I owe him lots and lots of chocolate. We're meeting tomorrow after school!

He had ignored me all week. Still sitting at different desks, walking right past me and stuff. But today, when he did it, I swear he glanced at me and seemed sad.

I really do hope he's OK.

I scraped together all my pocket money and some change my dad had in a jar in the entryway because he hates having cash on him. He has this thing about how nobody uses cash anymore but still gives me my pocket money in cash. Hypocrite much?

Anyway, that should be enough for one of each type of chocolate bar I can get at the shops. Or at least one of each that Mike can have. He's allergic to peanuts. Oh, and he hates coconut, so none with that.

Anyway, my plan is to head out early tomorrow and go to the shops on the way to school to buy as many chocolates as I can, then put them all into his locker. So glad we know each other's locker combinations!

Mike's combo is his birthday. Super original. He'll never work in cyber security or anything. But at least it makes it easy to remember.

I hope he likes the chocolates! I mean, I know he loves chocolate in general; I just hope it's not too much or anything. But given how annoyed he is, I'm not sure it will be enough.

Ugh, I'm finding it so hard to write. My hands are all shaking and stuff. I have no idea how I'm going to sleep tonight.

The school counsellor (and yes, I am talking about you if you ever read this) would probably tell me to do some mindfulness or something. I mean, that stuff is all over social media.

At least it's not as strange as some of the stuff that started showing up after everything changed. Some weird people decided that old "cures" must be real just because old folk tales were.

Like the Wesleyans, who follow this old guy who said that eating boiled carrots could cure asthma and that electricity cures basically anything. They've got a centre in almost every state now, and even have TV ads showing happy kids eating boiled carrots and playing. Like, what kid is ever happy eating boiled vegetables?

Though the Wesleyans aren't as weird as the Plinyists. They basically worship this guy called Pliny the Elder from back when Vesuvius erupted and killed everyone in Pompei. Pliny had some REALLY bizarre ideas, like helping babies relax by putting goat's poop near them, using goat's milk as toothpaste, and injecting goat pee into your ears to cure a stiff neck. I feel sorry for any goats near the Plinyists.

I don't know how they can believe anything from a guy who honestly said that bear cubs are born as white lumps of flesh that literally need to be "licked into shape" by their mothers. He also claimed there was an animal that was like a mix between a bull and a horse that sprayed flaming dung from its butt to attack.

Oh, and Pliny was also REALLY racist, but the modern Plinyists keep going with that line that he was "just a product of his time" and use that to ignore the blatant racism.

I hate that argument so much! Just because the racism is from a racist time doesn't mean we should refuse to recognise it and change systems so they're less racist.

OK, that went off on a weird tangent.

I'll admit it: I'm on edge. Knowing that I get to talk to Mike again tomorrow, but not being able to do anything right now.

Maybe I should try some of that mindfulness stuff?

Nah, I'll find a mindless game to play or something. I'm sure that's close enough.

16 JUNE

Oh. My. God.

OK, so today was HUGE!

I did the chocolate in the locker thing. And even though Mike still didn't sit with me in any of our shared classes today, he at least looked at me. And he seemed more sad than angry.

I kept wondering if he'd been to his locker yet. Surely he would have, right? I mean, if he'd gotten the chocolates already, why was he still acting the same?

Had I crossed a line again?

The day DRAGGED! Like, every class felt like an entire day. Lunchtime was even more awful than it had been the last few days. I went to the library and did some assignment work, which somehow made time feel faster rather than slower. While doing an assignment! It was weirdly good.

Well, except that Adriana was there. She spends a lot of time in the library. Thankfully she was over in the fantasy and sci-fi section, which is the farthest corner from the desks to work at, so I could keep her out of sight and mostly out of mind.

When school was finally over, I went to the park where Mike and I had agreed to meet. He wasn't there, but I was a few minutes early so I waited. And he still wasn't there.

I had destroyed almost all the grass near where I was sitting and was about to leave, sure Mike wasn't showing, but then he did! And he had the bag of chocolates in one hand and was eating one, so I took that as a good sign.

But something was wrong. Like, his hand was shaking even more than mine last night, to the point that it took him several tries to put the last of the bar into his mouth as he walked toward me.

He looked scared and somehow older. I have never seen him like that, not even when the change happened and he found out his dad was a dryad and his parents split.

I tried to act like things were normal, but he just looked at me. There is this way Mike can look with those dark brown eyes that just screams "Really??" in a way I haven't seen from anyone else. I would think that was a skill he got in the change, but he's had that as long as I can remember.

So yeah, that shut me up. All I could do was offer a hug, which he accepted.

That hug was so long that I would have been embarrassed if it had been at school. But we were alone, and I didn't care. Mike is my best friend and he obviously needed it. His whole body shook, and I heard him sob, but he tried to hide it, so I pretended it hadn't happened.

He was shaking so hard I had to support him, make sure he wouldn't fall down.

I was really scared. Had I hurt him that bad? I didn't think calling his dad would be so awful for him. I felt like my heart might explode from pain.

I helped him sit down, and he just sat there eating chocolate for a bit. He didn't talk, and I decided not to ask. I had made enough of a mess of things already.

Thankfully we sat slightly away from where I had been before, so there was more grass for me to destroy while Mike pulled himself together.

When he started talking, Mike just asked about that substitute teacher for Chemistry. But he didn't look at me when he spoke.

So I told him all about it. Then he asked how I was doing and how school was. I tried to go on as long as possible, but we eventually ran out of things to talk about. He still hadn't met my eyes.

My chest had started hurting again. There had clearly something going on that I had no idea about, but I didn't know how to approach it or what to do to make Mike feel better. I ended up just apologising again for contacting his dads and saying how bad I felt and that I would never do it again.

My eyes might have gotten a bit moist, but I definitely didn't cry.

Then Mike was hugging me again and saying it wasn't my fault, that it was all him, and that I'm a good friend.

I had never been more confused.

Slowly, with lots of pauses, Mike finally told me what was going on.

He wasn't annoyed with me because I called his dad. I mean, he was a bit, but that wasn't why he'd gotten so angry with me. He got mad because it was a distraction. Because he was trying not to think about something that had already made him so upset and confused that his head was spinning, which was only made worse when his dads came up with their plan to help him.

Mike thinks he somehow caused Mr. Dane's death.

The week before Mr. Dane died, the teacher had pulled Mike aside and said he was going to fail him because he obviously wasn't trying, even though Mike tries harder than anyone else! He hadn't told me about that, which hurt a bit, but that's not relevant right now.

Anyway, that night, Mike was writing in his school-mandated journal and was really angry and upset and ended up saying he wished Mr. Dane's shrivelled-up heart would finally give up on him so all the students would be put out of their misery.

And then, a few days later, it did.

Mike freaked out, thinking he had somehow caused it.

He's got some crazy theory about him being a new kind of Creature that we don't know about yet. He found an online forum about these Hindu demons called Asura. Supposedly they were sorcerer-like beings, filled with greed and ego, who thought it was fun to hurt other people and create chaos.

Why do mythical creatures always seem to have an awful sense of what's amusing?

So now Mike is convinced he's some kind of demon, and he caused Mr. Dane's death.

I tried to tell him that made no sense. There is no evidence that Asura even exist in India. Or at least, I had never seen anything on the Creature info website I subscribe to. And even if they did, there isn't a strong Hindu presence in our region to make him turn into one. And even if there was, and he was an Asura, it wasn't really his fault, right? Like when Dad accidentally killed Fluffy.

Mike didn't agree, no matter what I said. He's convinced he's to blame for Mr. Dane dying.

But he also can't tell anyone. He wants to tell the police, to hand himself in, but there's no knowing what would happen to him. It was bad enough before the change, being black. Who knows what they'd do to him once they discovered he was a demon?

Of course, I promised I wouldn't tell a soul. This journal doesn't count. I'll keep it hidden in the back of my closet, and I'd burn it before I let anyone read it, even the school counsellor.

After telling me all of that, Mike just seemed so exhausted. Like he hadn't slept for a week, which is probably not far from the truth. So I helped him home, reassuring him the whole way that he was wrong and it was a freak coincidence.

I mean, it has to be, right? My best friend isn't a demon! Mike is one of the nicest people I've ever met. I mean, the very fact that he's so upset by the idea that he could be a demon shows he couldn't be something evil, right?

I think he might have been slightly convinced by the time we reached his home. But maybe that's wishful thinking.

His lumberjack dad was waiting for Mike when we arrived. I think there might have been some moisture in his eyes when he saw us together. It was only a glimpse, though, before he put his hand over his face to comb his fingers through his beard. That thing is glorious: all amber curls, with some silver through it in these streaks that remind me of an orange badger.

Anyway, Mike and I agreed to do some online gaming tonight, and it's time for me to log in. I'm so glad to have my best friend back!

17 JUNE

Today was great! Even better than a regular Friday! Even getting a surprise English weekend assignment couldn't bring me down.

Mike and I sat next to each other in classes again, and at lunch.

I did a heap of research last night into the Asura, and I'm even more sure Mike isn't one. First, Asuras became that way because they were greedy and mean, which isn't Mike at all. Second, they are generally shown with multiple sets of arms. Unless Mike has been hiding them from me, he hasn't sprouted any more limbs.

Mike laughed at that, even though it was a terrible joke.

I'm not sure he believes me yet, but at least we're talking. And he's told someone how he's feeling. He hasn't told his dads yet, or the school counsellor, even though they're forcing him to do weekly visits.

I suggested maybe he should see a proper therapist. I mean, I know it wasn't my thing, but they have some confidentiality thing where they can't tell people that stuff, right? Maybe that would help.

Mike just gave me this look, as if saying: "Getting this from my dads is enough. You can shut up now."

So I did.

We had Chemistry this afternoon with the same substitute teacher, and Mike really got into the experiment. It was taking a sample of dirt from outside, isolating out the microplastics and identifying what type they were. I thought it was super depressing, but Mike loved how practical it was, how he could see where and why it would be used. Somehow that even made the maths seem easier for him, like he finally saw a reason to do it rather than just to get good grades.

That made me SO HAPPY.

The one thing that's still worrying me about Chemistry class is that Megan still isn't back. No one has heard from her since Mr. Dane died.

Surely she can't still be in custody. I mean, she didn't do it! And she's only a teenager. I mean, she's nowhere near the age of criminal adulthood, or whatever it's called. But when I've asked teachers about it, they tell me to mind my own business and let the police do what they need to do.

Well, not all teachers. Mrs. Lui got angry and quiet. But I guess, being a fellow pixie, she has feelings about what happened.

English has been a bit weird since that all happened, especially with Tanya still spreading rumours about how Megan killed Mr. Dane with some pixie powers that they've kept hidden.

She's made some disgusting comments about Mrs. Lui, about how she should go back to where she came from and not threaten us. Really gross stuff. I mean, Mrs. Lui came here as a refugee. And yeah, she's a pixie, but that just means she has wings and can fly short distances! Oh, and her eyes turned green, which I think looks sort of nice on her.

If anything, all the pixies I've heard talk about the transition have said it's a bit annoying because now they need to get their clothes tailored around their wings. And if they want to go somewhere quickly, it's much easier to drive than to fly, since the wings only let them hover above the ground a bit.

Not that I've heard much from the pixies since Mr. Dane died. They've been keeping to themselves, a group of winged backs to the world out on the oval during lunch. They're probably worried about the rumours that they have death magic, about what some people might do. There was a lot of that sort of stuff in the first few weeks after the change.

Anyway, back to the happy stuff!

Mike and I went to the shops after school and hung around for a bit. He has been thinking of getting something for his dads to say thanks for looking after him. Well, and to get them off his back.

He found an acorn necklace pendant for his dryad dad and some beard oil for his human dad. I didn't know beard oil was a thing, but it's not like I have a beard, and Dad shaves every day.

It felt good to hang out and go shopping for random stuff. Like old times, even before everything changed. Well, except that before it all changed, jewellery companies pretended stuff was silver, while now they have special ranges that look like silver but aren't, for the vampires and werewolves, that somehow cost more than the real thing.

Capitalism will always find a way to make money, right?

Which reminds me that I saw a new thing on the news tonight. Supposedly there's now a market in selling selkie seal skins, especially uni students trying to pay their way through their degrees. It's supposedly all consensual, so the selkie agrees to stay in human form as long as someone else has their seal skin. But that's still pretty gross if you ask me. I mean, they should have the choice, right? And if they need the money so badly that they'll sell off that choice, is it really consensual?

I've obviously been talking with Leigh too much. They have LOTS of thoughts about this sort of stuff, to the point that Leigh regularly has fights with our Dad about our society and the "class system" and say we need to change. They talk about some old guy called Marx, but I don't understand all of it.

But yeah, it was a great day. For a week that started so badly, I'm feeling terrific again. And looking forward to a weekend without worrying about my best friend.

22 JUNE

Things are still going well! It's like the world is making up for the awful few weeks.

I got a B on that surprise assignment for English. It seems Mrs. Lui liked my critique of *A Midsummer Night's Dream*. I thought it was odd having a pixie suggest we read that play of all the Shakespeare, but when I told Leigh about it, they said she probably wanted to point out how it was an awful way of depicting pixies/fairies.

So I wrote about everything Shakespeare got wrong about how pixies/fairies work, and Mrs. Lui loved it!

"Write to the audience," Leigh said. I guess they were right.

There's a lot I didn't realise, though. Like how fairies/pixies were used in medieval times to excuse people's awful behaviours. Yeah, it was a pixie that grabbed the barmaid's butt, not the drunk guy. As if.

Also, elves and fairies/pixies did not hang out together. And Shakespeare was the one who came up with them being small instead of human sized.

Oh, and the whole thing of Titania being the Queen of the Fairies was a way to get the English queen to like Shakespeare and give him money. Why does it always come back to money?

Anyway, a B is good for me, especially since I didn't give quite as much time to the assignment as I probably should have. But I'd just reunited with Mike, and there was SO MUCH gaming time to catch up on. And Shakespeare is boring!

Oh, on the topic of Shakespeare and boring, there was a big fuss at lunch today. And, of course, Ayan was involved.

He is so set on being some big stage actor that he pretends that "all the world's a stage" by making himself the main character whenever possible. Yeah, that's another line Ayan spouts all the time, so I guess it's also from Shakespeare or something.

But anyway, I need to backtrack. This morning, in the announcements on the PA, Mr. Rusico said that the school play was being scrapped. It was supposed to be *All's Well That Ends Well* because schools love Shakespeare and hate anything written in the last century that might actually be relevant.

Mr. Rusico said they had decided to cancel it "in light of Mr. Dane's untimely death". But it's supposed to be a comedy, so I'm not sure that's the reason. Couldn't we all use a bit of humour right now?

Anyway, Ayan DID NOT take the cancellation well.

We were having lunch. It was jambalaya, which is usually my favourite thing that the cafeteria puts on, but this one seemed particularly smoky. Or maybe they burnt something, because there was a bit of a haze in the air. The kitchen must be having issues, because it's been smoky often lately. Probably too cheap to change the oil in the fryers.

Anyway, the smoke was making my lungs tickle from asthma, so I was trying to force myself to breathe deeply when Ayan decided to do one of his infamous overacting spells in the middle of the cafeteria.

He was doing this back-and-forth thing, playing a bunch of characters. Because he's the only person so into this crap that he'd act it out in the middle of the cafeteria.

There was something about stealing and drunkenness, then talk of honesty, and another character talking about love. I only recognised one line: "A pox on him, he's a cat still."

I'd heard that before somewhere, but I never really got it. I mean, I like cats. They're really independent. Like, if a dog loves you, it's because they're a dog, but if a cat does, it's because you've earned it!

But I looked into it this afternoon, and Shakespeare seemed to have a massive issue with cats. Even though cats would have reduced the impact of the Black Plague in Shakespeare's time because they ate the rats that carried the fleas that spread it.

Not that he would have known that, I guess. Back then, they thought sickness was because of the wrong levels of bile, blood and phlegm in the body and they didn't know that germs existed. Weird, right?

Anyway, I know Ayan thinks he's known for his "performances", but it wasn't a smart move, given there were a few teachers in the room, including Ms. Hoxha. I saw her there, watching him while holding a ceramic plate and biodegradable cutlery, because she's far too fancy to use the usual cafeteria stuff. Ayan will probably get a few more counsellor sessions booked in, whether he likes it or not.

Better him than me, though. And certainly better than Mike. He REALLY doesn't like Ms. Hoxha for some reason, and he's already been through so much.

At least he seems to be starting to believe that Mr. Dane's death isn't his fault. He is still down sometimes, but nowhere near as much. And it's not like anything else he wanted has come true, so it's much more likely that he's just a normal human like me, right? I mean, if he were an Asura, surely he'd have beaten me in our latest gaming session!

And hey, he's really enjoying the new substitute teacher for Chemistry. He seems much more engaged and excited, though he still sometimes gets really quiet, as if it just hits him again.

He still hasn't finished all those chocolate bars. He even offered me some, but it felt weird taking them. I mean, it was my way of apologising, so wouldn't that be a bit like taking the apology back? I don't know.

Back to the play being cancelled: Mike said he overheard Mr. Rusico's EA say that there are termites in the school hall, and it will have to be closed and thoroughly fumigated, maybe even rebuilt. It wouldn't surprise me; that place hasn't been upgraded in about a century!

It's like so much of that place. It's falling apart. The last time I saw the school band perform, their drummer broke through the main drum during the performance. The library is so outdated that there's an atlas that still has the USSR in it. I had to ask Dad what that was, which led to a long and boring conversation about a war that was somehow cold even though it was over years, so during summer as well as winter.

And Megan was right about the chemistry labs, no matter what anyone says. The Bunsen burners could have been replaced with some of the newer coated versions without exposed iron composites.

The only place here that seems to be getting upgrades is the gym. They got the newest basketballs and footballs made with all-natural materials so druids can use them. I guess sport is always more important than getting an education, right?

Some people say it's because the school is trying to get Paul Azeri's parents to stay in town rather than move somewhere he can play higher-grade basketball. Paul's the best athlete we've had in town in decades, and he's wasted here, but the school wants the glory of being associated with him.

It seems that's pretty common, given how many students fawn over Paul. In the last few months alone, he's dated Daisy, Ayan, Tanya and Pete, and that's just the ones I know for sure. Anna talks about him CONSTANTLY, just because he's got muscles. Gross.

Though I guess he's done some other good stuff. I mean, he was the one who convinced the school to improve their relationship and consent education to include pan and ace people, rather than just straight, gay, or bi. But I still don't think that's enough to make up for him being a stupid jock most of the time.

So yeah, Mike thinks the play might have been cancelled because the hall will need all that work, but they don't want to tell us because it will look bad, so they're blaming it on Mr. Dane's death. That would make more sense.

But I doubt it will make Ayan any happier. Or any less likely to act out more stupid scenes written by a privileged white dude who's been dead for four hundred years. Who people think is all highbrow even though he made lots of fart jokes. I'd certainly never get even a B in English if I tried that!

Ugh, now I'm getting all worked up. I should stop, it's been a good day and I want to stay happy. Write again soon.

23 JUNE

OK, I know we should all be used to dealing with viruses and stuff these days, but smallpox?!

Yeah, Mr. Rusico has it! He's in the hospital, and we've all been sent into isolation. Like, not just the school, but the entire town!

The only people allowed to keep working are emergency services, healthcare services, garbage collectors, grocery store people (though it's no-contact delivery only), and a few others.

They even shut down the fast food and bottle shops this time! I think there will be lots of grocery orders of two-minute noodles for people who have no idea how to cook.

I mean, I know I'm not a great cook, but with how much Dad needs to work late, two-minute noodles became old fast once Leigh moved out. I've just been learning how to make mushroom stroganoff, and next I'm going to try this lentil curry stuff that Mike's dryad dad made one night while I was over there.

Anyway, back to the smallpox. (I NEVER thought I'd be writing that sentence.)

I heard from Mike, who heard from Tanya, who overheard some teachers talking, that Mr. Rusico started feeling a bit off yesterday afternoon. Standard stuff: fever, headache. But he still went out to dinner, even though he always tells us we're not allowed at school if we feel sick at all. The rumours say he was out with his receptionist on a secret date, but that seems far too cliché.

Anyway, the story goes that he suddenly vomited all over the table and got these red spots all over his face. Supposedly he started screaming at the waiter about how he was allergic to shellfish and they must have contaminated him or something. Then the spots started swelling into these pus-filled blisters and popping everywhere! Gross!

I sort of hope he was on a date and trying to be all suave and stuff, because that visual is hilarious. I mean, nasty, but still funny.

Not that I'm happy he's sick, of course.

So, he was taken to the hospital and they did all these tests. A few people were talking about it this morning, but no one took it that seriously until Vice Principal Abara came over the PA just before morning break and announced that Mr. Rusico had smallpox. Then everyone's phones started buzzing as we got an automated text message from the government announcing a state of emergency and ordering us all to immediately go home and stay there.

This was in Modern History, and Mr. Chastan, who is usually really strict about not having phones in class, didn't even get annoyed at us. He just started organising people to call parents or walk home if they lived nearby. He seemed in control, but his hand kept shaking, and I've never seen his eyes that wide.

Fun fact: Mr. Chastan became a dryad and has become friends with Mike's dad. His last name is French for "of the chestnut tree", but he is an oak dryad like most of them, which Mike thinks is ironic.

As Mike and I were leaving, alarms started blaring. I didn't know our town had community alert sirens. Surely the text message blast to everyone would have been enough without that annoying noise?

Anyway, I was looking up stuff about smallpox on the walk home because it's something I've vaguely heard of (in Modern History, coincidentally) but don't really know about. Which is because it supposedly got wiped out globally in 1979 by vaccination campaigns. And the symptoms usually come on over the course of days, not in one afternoon like what happened with Mr. Rusico.

Mike agreed that this is all super weird, but we didn't get a chance to talk about it before we had to go our separate ways home.

According to the news, the incubation period for smallpox can be over two weeks, so the council is trying to figure out how to react. I hope we're not in isolation for that long. A bit of time is great, but that long without seeing people? Between the COVID lockdowns and Dad keeping me at home for ages after the change, I've had enough social isolation for a lifetime!

Though, with how weird things have been lately, I am a happy not to have school for a bit. Should I feel guilty about that? I mean, Mr. Rusico is in intensive care and stuff. But I feel fine. And I'm sure he'll recover. They've got a hospital banshee to let them know if a person is about to die so they know who to prioritise, and the news says they haven't started screaming yet, so that's a great sign.

Supposedly Tanya saw some people in hazmat suits coming through town, but given she followed it up by telling Mike that her mother thinks they're here to implant people with microchips to track their movements, I don't know if that's true. And the local news website isn't reporting it yet.

Then again, they're all in isolation too, so they're probably finding it hard to report the latest details. According to the website, they've already petitioned the government for an exemption to the lockdown order so they can report on what's happening.

Dad got home only a few minutes after me and he's freaking out. Worried about what will happen in a week with the full moon if the werewolves can't do their usual cage companion thing. I told him not to worry, that they'll figure something out by then, or I can look after him, but he didn't listen to me. Typical adult.

I must admit it's strange, though. Like, how does a disease that was wiped out before my dad was even born suddenly show up in this nothing town?

And the second adult at the school to have something happen to them suddenly within a few weeks?

I'm sure Leigh would tell me it's just a coincidence. That there's no such thing as fate or curses or anything like that. But who would have believed that half the population would become folklore critters overnight? We still have no idea how that happened or what else could happen.

OK, so maybe I am a bit scared. This is all so weird, just when I thought I was finally getting used to weird.

I posted about it on the forum I follow for Creature news, and they're all really interested. One said something about it being the Nosoi, demons that escaped from Pandora's box. That led to an argument about whether Pandora had a box or an amphora and whether the difference mattered. I ignored that part.

A few people suggested gods like Shiva, Ra, Apollo or Chalchiuhtotolin. But there has been no evidence of gods coming to life, so they got shot down quickly.

So yeah, no one seems to know what's going on. And there have been no other reports of this happening elsewhere.

For once, this pathetic little town is getting national news. I even heard it's been covered overseas because it's so strange to have a smallpox outbreak out of nowhere. There are rumours that there's a hidden biological warfare lab in town, which is just stupid. I mean, I WISH this place was that interesting.

But I guess, for now, we just wait and see what happens. And see if anyone else gets sick.

In the meantime, a game Mike and I have been playing has a new storyline release due in two days, so that should keep us busy!

I guess I should get some homework and assignments done before then. Even as they were telling us all to go home, they said they still expected us to submit our assignments, which I think is rude.

That can wait for tomorrow, though. For tonight, there's a new show that's been released where people who were turned into Creatures wake up to find they're just human again, but it's only a few people, and they're trying to pretend nothing has changed. It looks so awful it might just be good. And it was a full-season drop, so I'm set for tonight!

24 JUNE

I am officially the worst friend ever. I didn't even realise until I was chatting to Mike this morning that he might think he caused Mr. Rusico's smallpox.

I thought he was over that "thinking he's a demon" thing. But all this stuff has brought it back up, and now he's trying to figure out if he ever said or thought anything bad about Mr. Rusico.

I feel awful. I was telling Mike all the theories I'd read online, both on the critter forum and the school chat, and he was so quiet, and I don't even know how long I was talking before I realised.

It's not like he had anything against Mr. Rusico, right? He was failing Chemistry, but the principal wasn't involved yet. And he wasn't in any other trouble.

So I hadn't even thought that Mike would blame himself.

He shouldn't, right?

I mean, the whole idea of him being an Asura is stupid. They don't exist. Then again, vampires exist. And druids, and muses, and so many other things.

But there's no reason for an Asura to exist here. They're a Hindu demon, and there aren't many Hindus around here, right? I mean, there are some immigrants from India from the time of the Partition, but that doesn't necessarily mean they're Hindus, right?

I'm sure he's not a demon. Not Mike. He couldn't be. He's too nice.

That's what I told him. He pretended to believe it, but he didn't. I know him too well.

I don't know what to do. What if my best friend really is causing all this stuff to happen? Giving people heart attacks and smallpox? How do I even try to process that?

I have no idea.

25 JUNE

The last couple of days have been SO BORING! Like, I even ended up doing all my homework and assignments yesterday because I needed SOMETHING to do!

That show about Creatures who turned back to humans was even worse than I expected, but not in the way that made it good, just that made it even worse. I couldn't get through the third episode. I ended up watching nature documentaries I've already seen because at least it was something, and I've watched everything else interesting on our streaming services.

And we're not allowed out of the house. Not even into the yard.

Cops and official-looking vans are driving around, and the news says the council has started a program of testing EVERYONE in town. Like, people in hazmat suits going door to door, demanding people do a blood test to check for smallpox.

Supposedly they set up some special lab on the school oval in these giant plastic marquees and stuff, just like something from a movie. Except, of course, I can't go out to have a look. Even journalists aren't allowed to. Their request for an exemption got denied, so they're just relying on what the council is telling them and the official photos. Which, if online forums have taught me anything, is probably only a tiny part of what's really going on.

For example, the council keeps saying the program is going smoothly, encouraging us to all wait our turn to give our blood test. They didn't say anything about Tanya's mother refusing to give blood. Tanya posted about it on the school forum, repeating that stupid stuff her mother said about how they're testing people to collect their DNA and put in microchip trackers for some breeding program. Tanya's mother says a LOT of weird things, and Tanya sadly believes most of them.

Anyway, supposedly Ms. Jones slammed the door in the face of the people in hazmat suits and refused to open it again. So they called the police, who threatened to break down the door and force them to take the test.

At that point in telling the story, Tanya started going on about how they can't do that because of the Constitution, but I ignored that part.

But maybe she was right, because the cops didn't storm in. They've just been outside all day, watching the house. At least, according to Tanya.

I'm surprised they can spare the people. There seem to be cops everywhere, driving around to ensure no one is outside when they shouldn't be. And according to a forum I'm on, they've also got drones scanning for movement.

I feel like I'm in one of those sci-fi movies when the world has gone to crap, and there's some dictator in charge of everything. But at the same time, I totally get that smallpox is scary based on all the stuff I've read. It's not like people get immunised against it anymore because they thought it was gone.

The testing started on the other side of town, so the council thinks it will be a couple of days before they get to my place.

Oh, and last I heard, Mr. Rusico was stable but still in the ICU.

Supposedly they've got a healing elf there with him. It's a rare thing for elves to have. The theory is that the ability to heal only shows up occasionally in elves because only some of the folklore says they can heal.

Because they're so rare, they usually don't send them to small towns like ours, but I guess smallpox made us important enough.

I once heard that the US President has a whole team of healing elves just in case they get sick. Sounds about right, hoarding something that could help so many people.

Dad keeps checking in on how I'm going, with that worried parent "you can tell me anything" face that is SO ANNOYING. So, I'm sort of avoiding him.

With all my assignments done, I even cleaned my room, because at least I could tell Dad I was too busy doing that to talk. I might need to do a spring clean of the kitchen if this goes on much longer. What is happening to me?

At least it's only an hour until that game update gets released. I should grab something for lunch and some snacks, so I don't have to worry about taking a break to get food.

26 JUNE

The testers got here today, two of them. I swear, they had on the hazmat stuff that you see in movies! Except the suit was white, not yellow. And the masks were different: transparent all the way around but all puffed up like a balloon or some weird alien version of those blow-up people outside car dealerships.

They had the light blue medical gloves from the shows, but with this silver stuff around their wrist. It looked like duct tape.

The funniest part was that they were wearing these headphones inside the suit that came under the ear with a bulb-looking microphone, the type that pop stars wear in concerts. It made them look a bit like the weirdest J-pop band in history!

They didn't even introduce themselves. One started by reading out the public health order, under which we were "obligated by law" to "provide all appropriate samples" to determine whether we had been infected. While that was happening, the other one set up their supplies on the coffee table in the living room.

They refused to talk about what they'd discovered. While they were sucking blood out of Dad's left arm, I kept asking if they'd found any other smallpox cases, what was going on, if they knew how it got here, anything. But they were just silent. Didn't even look at me until they were done with Dad.

After Dad got up, the one taking blood gestured at me with a syringe in this super creepy way until I sat down in the chair and pulled up my sleeve.

They finally talked to me, but only to confirm my full name and date of birth and compare it to this sheet on a clipboard that they held angled so I couldn't see it. I was about to say something snarky, but Dad gave me one of his "not now" looks. So, I just gave the details and put out my arm.

They were NOT the best vampire nurse. And yes, I know, Daisy says it's "not appropriate" to use that term for the nurses that take blood, that it's discriminatory against vampires, but I don't care what Daisy thinks.

I just looked at my arm and it has already started to bruise.

After taking the blood, they just left. Not another word, just a nod of the head.

Dad went straight back into doing work. His boss has him working remotely. They couldn't even give him a few days off with potential smallpox around!

Damn capitalists. They only adopted full moon leave after a few werewolves got held back at work in factories and other big workplaces despite their pleas to go home, and things did not end well for the other employees.

Anyway, I had nothing else to do and Mike wasn't online yet, so I went looking to see if there was any news.

Everyone in the school group chat is still talking about Mr. Rusico. We got an email reminding us that we're only supposed to use that forum to talk about schoolwork, as if that will stop the rumours. But it's really just people giving their theories about what's happening to the principal.

There's the usual conspiracy stuff going around online in the local social media pages and forums. They've moved from the idea of a secret lab in town to it being a bio-attack from some enemy country. It was just like that when everything changed, everyone blaming other people and nations.

Not that there are as many enemy countries as before. Most of them took a break to come to grips with the change, or decided to wage war on the changed instead of other countries. There are a bunch of human rights organisations (they haven't figured out what name to change to yet, given it's not just humans now that they're representing) calling out violations. But the UN doesn't seem to know what to do, so they're staying out of it. Saying it's up to each country to handle how they "integrate" populations in our "new normal".

I'm so sick of new normals. Why can't normal just be normal?

Anyway, that's one of the theories. The Nosoi idea is pretty popular too. Someone mentioned the "plague hags" that have shown up in a few cultures. I think that was a bit off, and they definitely need a new name for that myth. Surely everyone knows now that the term "hag" is awful and denigrating to women (and yes, Leigh taught me all that stuff and the word "denigrating").

What no one can figure out is why Mr. Rusico would be targeted. I mean, he's mostly harmless. Apart from a few suspensions here and there, and terrible fashion taste, he isn't that bad.

The rumour about him being on a date with his receptionist turned out to be a lie. I mean, it was "a" receptionist, but not his, and it seems to have been a legit date. Which is almost as gross an idea as the smallpox pustules.

But anyway, why would any critter give Mr. Rusico smallpox? So far, there have been no official reports of anyone else getting it, and I can think of much worse people.

Which always seems to bring up Mr. Dane. He WAS one of those bad people, and he died. So maybe Mr. Rusico actually is too, but has hidden it? I mean, we've all heard of those people. They are the "normal person next door" who "never had a bad word against anyone" until people find out they're a serial killer with bodies buried in their backyard or bricked into walls.

Yes, I might have watched a few true crime documentaries. Like EVERY other person on Earth. Doesn't mean I'm wrong, right?

Because it's definitely not Mike.

28 JUNE

We're all clean! The whole town. No smallpox anywhere except for Mr. Rusico, and he didn't even spread it to the receptionist date or hospital staff. And I hear he's recovering.

I never thought I'd enjoy just going into my backyard this much. Dad wouldn't let me go any further, which is stupid, but he didn't trust the SMS we got from the council. Said he'll wait until "formal advice" as if a text message isn't formal enough.

But just breathing fresh air felt so good!

I'm writing this while outside. It's dark, but I turned on the spotlights. Some moths keep flittering around in the light. Also mosquitoes, which I am NOT OK with.

Dad still refuses to come out. He's not happy I'm here, but I just needed it.

On the topic of Dad, he's all paranoid about the full moon coming up. He has asked Leigh to come back for a few days to "look after" me. As if I need looking after??

But it will be so good to see Leigh. I haven't seen them in months. Since they went off to uni, it's been only the occasional video call. And I swear Dad has gotten more protective, as if he's used all the protectiveness of two kids and given it all to me.

It's uni break, so Leigh will be visiting for a few days. No idea what they'll do to occupy their time in this sleepy town after the joys of living in the city, but I'm sure we'll find something.

Just because I'm excited to see Leigh doesn't mean I'm not annoyed at Dad, though. He actually said he doesn't want "just a babysitter" looking after me, given everything that's happened.

I told him I can look after myself, but he just gave me that look where there's no expression on his face, like he didn't hear a word I said. Then he went on to talk about how Leigh was arriving as soon as the "formal" announcement was made to allow people to visit, so hopefully they'll be here tomorrow with plenty of time before the full moon on Thursday.

No word yet on when we have to go back to school. Hopefully they will give us the rest of the week off. I mean, with all the fear we've been under, surely we deserve that?

29 JUNE

They didn't give us the rest of the week off.

We all had to go back to school today, even though the official word only came through just before 9 p.m. last night. And we had to spend the first period in a session on "coping with stress" led by the school counsellor.

She held it outside, which was not ok! It was a cold morning, all misty and stuff, and we were all shivering outside in big jackets. Except for my cousin Anna and Ms. Hoxha.

I understand Anna being fine with it. Even in human form, selkies have this thing where they're better at being cold. I guess it comes from being part seal? Or because they're supposed to have been comfortable in icy seas and stuff?

Regardless, she was wearing a t-shirt even while the rest of us were shivering, and looking all smug about it. She's even started putting her hair in long blond plaits down the front, pretending to be engaging with her "Norse heritage" or something.

But Ms. Hoxha also seemed fine. Maybe she's a lizard person and cold-blooded? Actually, that means she'd hate the cold, right? I was never good at biology.

Anyway, she did all that standard counselling stuff. Talking about mindfulness and "making sure our cups are full". Encouraged us to keep writing in these journals and visit her if we had any thoughts we needed to discuss.

She went through it quickly, like she just wanted it to be over as much as all the rest of us did. Maybe she was actually cold but hid it well?

While she talked, her eyes kept sweeping over us. They seemed a bit more brown with a hint of green in the dim light, while they're usually a brighter hazel in her office.

I swear, those eyes feel like they pierce right into you. Maybe that's something they teach counsellors as part of the degree? That and the head tilt.

Anyway, thankfully, she was done quickly.

Then Vice Principal Abara did a speech about being aware of "rumours" circulating about what happened to Mr. Rusico and how it was "inappropriate" for students to be "engaging in such supposition". I guess they discovered the stuff on the forums. But I made sure not to use my real name, unlike most people there. I mean, you never know who's online!

Mx. Abara didn't talk long and we moved back inside as the mist was clearing, just in time for second period.

I saw Adriana on the walk in. Her nose was bright red and she was sniffling and shivering. Her parents insist on her wearing a skirt instead of pants, and long socks instead of tights, so her legs must have been freezing! Why can't they just let her be? What deity wants Adriana to suffer so that she conforms to some outdated notion of femininity?

Oh, yeah, I sound like Leigh. Who is coming home tonight! They should be here within an hour, just in time for dinner.

I wonder how Dad will respond to their hair. I saw online that they dyed it bright blue last week, but I haven't told Dad. It really suits them.

I hope he's OK with it. If so, maybe I can do something cool with mine! He'll never let me get a piercing. Supposedly I'm not allowed to "mutilate" myself under his roof.

As far as I know, he's never commented on Leigh's septum piercing. He just pointedly ignores that it exists, which Leigh finds hilarious. So, of course, Leigh swaps from the subtle silver ring they usually wear into an oversized clicker with gems when they visit.

Don't get me wrong, Leigh loves Dad. They just also love teasing him about being old-fashioned. And somehow, they can get away with it when I wouldn't dare. But I have to live with him!

I wonder if Dad was this conservative when he was a teenager. I heard someone say you get more conservative as you get older. I am NOT going to let that happen to me.

Anyway, the only other thing to report from school today is that Megan is back. Supposedly the cops finally decided she didn't kill Mr. Dane, but she won't talk about where she was or what she was doing over the last three weeks. All day, even in classes, she just hung out with the other pixies, who wouldn't let anyone come near her.

She looked drawn and tired, which was a bit shocking. As long as I've known her, Megan seemed full of fire, even when her body started failing and she was diagnosed with juvenile arthritis.

She always had a cause of some kind that she's been passionate about, this internal energy. Even when I disagreed with her position, I liked that about Megan. She has purpose.

But today she just seemed … flat. Like something had turned off the light inside her. Her eyes still shone green, but that's a pixie thing. It wasn't the same.

And she was using her rollator rather than the cane. I've only seen her use that once before, when she was recovering from glandular fever.

I hope she's OK. If we were closer, I would have checked in on her, but at least she has the other pixies to look after her.

I overheard Tanya talking about it, saying awful stuff about them allowing a killer back at school, so I told her to shut up. But she's not the only one. Even Daisy made comments over the video link at lunch. Stuff about the school standards dropping and how her father was looking into options for a "safer" learning environment.

She's not even physically here! And she's a vampire. It's not like much can kill her, and she has super quick healing.

Adriana called Daisy out on that one. It was pretty surprising, because Adriana hates speaking in front of crowds. But maybe her recent change in fortune has made her more confident? I hope so. So yeah, she basically said that if the school can accommodate literal and figurative blood suckers, they can take in innocent people too. Burn!

I felt so proud of Adriana, I nearly burst. Like, I grabbed Mike's hand under the table and we just looked at each other and then at Adriana and then started clapping! A few others in the cafeteria joined in, but the look on Daisy's face stopped the rest.

She was ready to kill! It looked like she was trying to come up with some comeback, but then her screen went black, so she must have logged off.

Then everyone joined us in applauding Adriana, who turned bright red. Although she was "properly" covered up as usual, I swear she was blushing all the way down to her toes!

I tried to go up to congratulate her, but too many others were mobbing her. Including Paul Azeri. I overheard someone saying he'd broken up with his last partner during the lockdown and is trying to get with Adriana.

I am not jealous about that. I mean, even if I felt a weird twing, there is NO WAY her parents would let Adriana date anyone, so there was nothing to be jealous about.

They also won't let her have a mobile, so I couldn't text her, so I sent her an email. Archaic, right? But a few minutes later she was on her school laptop, and she looked up at me and smiled. That was really lovely, but it reminded me how much I miss seeing that gorgeous smile. The way one side goes up just a moment before the other.

I really should make an effort to get in touch with her again. See how she's going with the whole "being a muse" thing and suddenly being popular.

Hopefully she responds to the email and we can start chatting again. That would be really nice.

OK, Leigh should be here any minute now, so I am going to get the last of my homework done.

29 JUNE...AGAIN

OMG, I had forgotten how awesome Leigh is! Or maybe they've just gotten more awesome since they went to university. I didn't get a chance to see them in person through the change, since travelling was risky and Dad was all concerned, and they've only been able to get away from their studies a few times since.

Leigh made so many snarky comments over dinner. I mean, nice snarky. The playful kind that means you love the person but also enjoy annoying them just a bit.

As we were sitting down, they said they were going to ask if Dad was seeing anyone, but the sweater vest he was wearing and the side-part haircut made it clear that wasn't happening any time soon. Dad blushed so hard and blubbered, trying to respond. I'm sort of glad he didn't really respond, though. I DO NOT need the idea of Dad dating. Gross!

Anyway, then Dad kept trying to be civil and even complimented Leigh's hair, but it was so obvious he was annoyed by the massive septum clicker they had in. It was a huge gold filigree thing with a garnet in the middle, and it sometimes shifted when they talked. So at one point, Leigh stopped, a fork of mashed potatoes halfway to their mouth, and said, "Didn't your dad teach you that staring is rude? Mine did."

I laughed so hard I got mash up my nose!

Dad did NOT think it was that funny. He gave me a massive glare for laughing, and I tried really hard to hold it in, but then Leigh gave me this look that said, "Isn't it funny when he's mad?" and I just couldn't!

Dad tried to give back, but he is SO BAD at it. He said something about how it wasn't funny how much he was paying to help Leigh through university when his dad didn't. Then Leigh clapped back with the statistics of how much more university and living costs are now than when Dad was young and how it was because his generation ruined it all.

I did stand up for Dad a bit then. I mean, it's not like Dad is a boomer. Leigh literally shuddered when I said the B-word.

Then they said, "Yeah, if I was raised by a boomer, I'd probably be super boring and spend my time on Facebook and LinkedIn." Then they looked right at Dad!

I mean, Leigh's not wrong. But maybe they were being just a bit harsh.

Dad isn't too bad. I mean, yeah, he complains about "adulting" sometimes, but it's not like he tries to pretend he's cool like some of my teachers or Daisy's dad. Mr. Smith came to a school play in ripped skinny jeans and a T-shirt from some old band he used to play in! And he kept trying to talk to people as if he was still our age. It was gross. Doesn't he know that having money doesn't automatically make you popular anymore?

Anyway, dinner went on like that. Dad made a comment about Leigh just being salty because they had to be at family dinner instead of streaming Netflix. It was so cute that he tried to join in the friendly insults. But then Leigh responded that they were more annoyed they were being called away from their side hustle making fan videos for old weirdos to raise money to promote queer rights.

I swear, Dad's eyes doubled in size, and Leigh had to assure him they don't do that! I think Leigh felt bad about that: they didn't even use it as an excuse to ask Dad to send them more money.

I've really missed Leigh. They are just so much fun, and they know how to play with Dad just enough without being too insulting. Every time I've tried that, I've had to go without my phone for a night. But Leigh promises I'll get the hang of it.

After dinner, Leigh and I caught up about everything that's been happening. About Mr. Dane and Mr. Rusico.

They said some things about Mr. Dane that I probably shouldn't write down, in case Dad or someone else ever reads this. They hated the guy too, even though he treated them better than most. Seems like that was pretty universal.

But Leigh did feel bad about Mr. Rusico. "He's harmless," they said. "A teddy bear, down to the belly and poorly fitting suit."

Not sure if I'd describe him that way. But now I keep thinking of him with fluffy teddy bear ears and a bow around his neck instead of a tie.

Leigh kept asking about Adriana, though. They seemed weirdly focused on how I feel about her being a muse. And no matter how many times I said I was so happy for her and stuff, Leigh kept giving me this "look". They have this way of looking that feels like you've been stabbed right into the brain, and you just want to escape but can't.

I eventually had to distract them by talking about what Mike is going through and how he thinks he's a demon. I know I promised not to tell anyone, but Leigh doesn't count, right? And I swore them to secrecy.

Leigh agrees that it's highly unlikely, and that even if Asura existed, Mike is far too nice to be one.

Even though I was sure about it anyway, having Leigh be so certain too was good.

Anyway, I need to get to bed now, before Dad comes up to check if the light is still on.

Tomorrow is a full moon, so hopefully Leigh and I can have some fun while Dad's caged up in the basement. Which would have been a REALLY weird sentence less than a year ago.

30 JUNE

Leigh and Dad picked me up from school, and it was great to spend all afternoon with them, even if there wasn't anything to do. This is a boring town usually, and the whole smallpox scare has all the old folks too scared to do much, so even some stores are closed.

You'd think they'd be able to adapt after everything that's happened lately. Leigh thinks people reach thirty and something happens in their brain that makes them incapable of being interesting anymore.

I know that was supposed to be a joke, but I don't think I've met a single person over 30 who was interesting. All they want to do is listen to the music that was popular when they were my age and complain about work. But at least that's better than people over 50 who complain about "young people these days". So many of them seem to think they don't need to be nice to others because people weren't so "delicate" when they were young. But we know so much more now, so of course things are different.

The only exciting thing from today was running into a horde of reporters outside the council building. Now that people can come into town again, there are journalists and cameras from lots of media outlets, from the leftist ones Leigh likes down to those tabloid types who will probably find some way to make Mr. Rusico getting smallpox into some kind of sex scandal.

I don't get their obsession with making everything about sex. I know, I'm a teenager: sex is supposed to be a big thing to me, according to all the teachers at school. But adults make almost everything about sex, more than anyone in my grade, and I don't get why.

I told Leigh that, and they asked if Dad had tried to have "the talk" with me. Seems he had it with Leigh when they were my age. I'm not sure if I should be glad that he hasn't or insulted.

Anyway, there were camera crews everywhere outside the council building. All these people from around town were standing around, trying to get into the background of some footage, and I thought it was pathetic. Who cares if you're in the background of some news story that has nothing to do with you?

Then Leigh walked up to the crowd, and I got confused. I mean, they're better than that, right? Because yeah, they are.

They walked right in front of a journalist in the middle of a live broadcast, looked at the camera and went on this massive tirade about how people only care when it's a white person that gets smallpox "when the media still doesn't discuss the horrors of how smallpox destroyed entire civilisations in the Americas", and that they should be "covering the fight for equal rights for the queer community, people of colour and other marginalised groups instead of wasting time in this no-name town trying to get ratings".

I did not cry at how awesome that was. Nope. I just got a bit of hay fever or something. It happens in seasons other than spring!

But Dad teared up, which surprised me a bit. I had expected him to stop Leigh. But when Leigh was done, they walked back to us and Dad just gave them this massive hug.

I think he said something, but I couldn't hear it. And when he let Leigh go, his eyes were all glassy and he kept blinking.

Leigh blushed and made a comment about Dad not being so bad sometimes.

Then Dad decided to take us to get ice cream. He NEVER takes me for ice cream, so he must have been pleased with what Leigh did. Maybe Leigh is correct, and Dad is better than I give him credit for.

Then again, he asked Leigh to visit because he doesn't trust me on my own on a full moon. He wouldn't even let me help secure him in the cage, but made me stay in my room while Leigh and one of Dad's usual werewolf carers did it.

Werewolf care is a whole part-time gig these days. The hours are lousy, being only one night a month, but they also advise on cages and restraints throughout the month.

I remember Megan suggesting it was too easy for werewolves to get human-sized cages and restraints so quickly after the change, but that is NOT something I want to think about associated with my dad.

On that, I should probably check how Megan is doing on Monday. I sent her a message on the school chat yesterday, but she hasn't replied.

Once Dad was all caged up and night fell, Leigh and I sat around watching shows and chatting. It sounds like they're doing well at uni. They talked about lots of friends and the groups they're in.

I'm glad they finally found a place they are accepted for the incredible person they are. Not like in this town. I know Dad tried to shield them from some of the worst stuff, but people talk. Especially when it's about people who are different from them.

Then again, maybe things are better now? People are so much more different in more ways now, and we're somehow coping with that.

Around 9 p.m., Dad's howls got so loud that Leigh and I sometimes had to shout to hear each other. I'm not sure if I'll ever get used to my father howling at a full moon and probably chasing his tail, then tomorrow acting as if he's just a typical dad who can tell me what to do.

I asked Leigh if I should buy him a chew toy or something, but they think that crosses a line. Then they said I should start with some dried beef ear treats and see how he feels about that first.

I'm sure that was a joke, but I am SO tempted!

Dad doesn't remember much of what happens when he's a wolf. He tried to tell me about it once and said it was like living in strobe lighting, so you only see little bits of what happens and have to piece the rest together. At the same time, it's like a dream when you know you're not yourself, you're someone else and you sort of know your backstory, but when you wake up you can't remember that part, only that you weren't yourself and did things you wouldn't do.

Sounds weird. I'm glad I'm not a werewolf.

I'm also glad I'm not a banshee or a valkyrie. The valkyrie have been THE WORST at school. Combining their mood swings and extraordinary fighting skills with puberty hormones has NOT been fun. At least we've only had a few hospitalisations, unlike many places where things have been worse.

I asked Leigh what they would be if they could choose any of the critters instead of staying human. After correcting my use of the term "critter", they said a muse, which I agree would be cool because they get paid so much. But Leigh said it was because they wanted to spend their life inspiring people, giving them ideas that make the world a better place.

I'm sure they want the money too, even if they claim to be a socialist and say that money is just a way to control the workers. I mean, money makes the world work, right?

Anyway, when Leigh said that, it made me think about Adriana again.

Leigh is the only person I told about how I felt about Adriana, back before her parents caught me trying to kiss her. They said I should tell Adriana how I felt, which I had planned to do the day I kissed her, so I didn't want to talk about it.

Instead, I said I wished I was a vampire, because drinking blood isn't that bad for getting to live forever and being basically unkillable.

Yeah, I know, that was a poor move, since Leigh is vegan and big on animal rights. They got all grossed out, and I feel a bit bad. But I needed to do something to change the topic.

Things felt a bit weird after that, so I came back upstairs and here I am, writing in this stupid journal.

I don't know why I'm still doing this. It's not like it's helping, or that I need help. Everything is fine.

It's just because school said I should. That's all.

1 JULY

Leigh left tonight to go back to uni. It was so nice to have them here. I wish they'd visit more often, but I probably won't see them for months since it's a nearly three-hour drive away.

They promised to keep up our weekly chats online, but they get distracted a lot and forget, so we usually only catch up every few weeks. They mean well, but between studies and their new friends and clubs and stuff, they lose track of time and have other things on.

Anyway, I managed to talk to Megan in Chemistry today, but she didn't say much other than claiming to be fine. She still seems off to me, like she's scared of saying or doing anything. Even her wings seem smaller, like they wilted or something, and she's still using the rollator.

I mean, she's had issues since the juvenile arthritis started, but this seems bigger.

I wish I knew what the cops did to her. Then again, maybe I don't want to know.

Should I support her more? It's not like we're close, and she has her group of pixies. But she doesn't seem to be any better today than she was last week.

Was that look a cry for help? Or did she just want me to go away? I don't know!

Anyway, not much else went on today. I got out of Maths for my monthly counsellor session, which was much like all the others.

Ms. Hoxha kept asking how I felt about being stuck at home for so long while they were checking the town for smallpox. Whether I was angry at anyone for it.

She seems to assume I'll be angry at people all the time. I mean, yeah, I'm a teenager, I get annoyed and stuff. But it's like she thinks the hormones are turning us all into serial killers in the making and she's here to help us become stereotypical adults. Typical of her generation, thinking we're the ones with all the problems when they're much more likely to be mass shooters! I'm just waiting for her to blame video games for "the way society is today". Would be so typical of adults.

So I told Ms. Hoxha the truth, that there's no one I'm angry at. Then she turned to asking about how Mike is going, which really annoyed me.

But I wasn't angry. Just annoyed. I mean, I'm not going to tell her stuff about Mike! That's his to talk about if he wants to.

Then she asked to read from this journal again. I decided to read her select parts of it, to make her happy, but avoided anything I'd written about her or Mike.

I did read out some of the stuff about how I felt about Mr. Dane, though. How I'd felt that night and the next day. I figured that would appease her that I was doing this thing right.

Anyway, the patchouli incense started making me sneeze around then, so she let me go early. She wanted to hold onto this journal to read more, but I said I needed to write in it tonight.

I guess I can pretend to be into this whole thing, at least to get Ms. Hoxha off my back. It's not like I need counselling. I just need school to settle down for a bit. It's surprisingly hard to concentrate on homework when teachers are dying and getting lethal diseases!

4 JULY

I don't know how to feel today. Like… what to believe. Or what to do. What should I do??

I guess I should backtrack. Ms. Hoxha said writing things down helps to process stuff, so just write it down in the order things happened and it will help.

Here goes.

It was lunchtime. Really nice day, so Mike and I took our lunch outside and sat on the oval. There was nothing special about it. We do that regularly, and lots of others were too.

The sun was warm and the air smelled of cut grass because the groundskeeper was mowing. I remember thinking of how I love that smell.

Mike and I were talking about random stuff. He was happy because he'd gotten a B– on the latest chemistry quiz, which brought him up to a pass overall. We spoke about how Megan was doing, and how I'm worried about her. Mike said he'd heard Tanya's still spreading rumours about

Megan, but everyone knows that's just her being Creaturist and is ignoring it.

Tanya must be glad she didn't turn into anything, with her mother being like that. Who knows what would have happened? I've heard a bunch of stories of kids being kicked out by their parents when they changed because they were considered evil or something. It's so awful. I mean, they didn't choose to become something other than human. None of us got a choice.

There are all these charities and refuges now for changed teens, and a massive campaign seeking foster parents that can be matched to a teen of the same Creature type to help guide them.

I wonder if it's easier being a teen or a child through all of this. I mean, if you were just in preschool and this happened, that could really mess you up if you don't understand what's going on. Imagine being a vampire toddler, or their parent!

I'm getting side-tracked.

I don't want to write this. But I think I need to.

So yeah, it was a beautiful day. Birds were squawking in the pine trees at the edge of the oval. Then something must have spooked them, and a whole flock of crows took flight at the same time and screeched off.

I remember watching a show a while back that said a group of crows is called a murder. At the time, I thought it was funny.

Anyway, when I heard the crows, I looked over that way so I saw the groundskeeper's reaction. Saw that he was freaked out by the birds flying off.

He stared at them, then turned, his eyes all wide and weird, looking at the sky all around. He was on the other side of the oval, so I didn't hear if he said anything, but his mouth was moving.

He kept spinning around and around, looking, then stopped suddenly. Then he launched himself at the ground.

You know, you never think about the little animals that are everywhere. You might think of mice, flies, or mosquitoes because they're annoying. But not so much of things like geckoes, bats, or moths that live their lives around us, not doing any harm. Just being themselves and ignoring us humans (and other things).

So, when the groundskeeper came up, he was holding a lizard of some kind in his greenish hand. It was too far away to see what it was, but it was skinny and around as long as my foot, including its tail.

He slammed it down on the mower, then held it in place while he pulled a knife off his tool belt. Then...

That's about when someone screamed. I don't know who it was because I couldn't stop looking at the groundskeeper.

I didn't know lizards have blood that looks just like human blood. For some reason, I thought it should look different, given how weird lizards are compared to us. Like, blue or something for being cold-blooded. But no, it's red. And there's a lot of it.

By the time some teachers had gotten to him, the groundskeeper had already done his ritual.

I knew he was a druid from the green tint to his skin. It's not a common change, which is good since they can't stand "unnatural" things like most of our homes. That's why he uses an old-fashioned metal mower instead of a newer plastic one. And I heard he lives in a timber cabin in the woods a few blocks from school.

I'd also heard some druids have the gift of prophecy if they do the right rituals. I just didn't know the ritual required intestines.

If anything, his eyes were even wider while the teachers dragged him toward the main school building, where the principal's office is. He was stumbling along, one teacher on each side as they tried to steer him away from the students, maybe hoping we wouldn't hear.

But I heard.

"The muse will die," the groundskeeper cried over and over.

I just realised I don't even know his name. He's always just been "the groundskeeper". But surely he has a name.

I ran to the library. Didn't even say anything to Mike, now that I think of it. Just left my stuff there and ran. Because that's where Adriana often spends her lunch break. It's where she feels safe.

The librarian tried to stop me as I ran in. I know, I'm not supposed to run inside. But I just didn't care.

I ran past the desk, up the stairs, to the section with the fantasy books that Adriana never lets her parents know that she loves, because they would think them the work of the devil or something.

And there she was. The sunlight coming through the window behind the bench seat she was sprawled on shone on her blond hair. It was a bit frizzy from the humidity outside, which made it look like a halo around her head.

I skidded to a stop in front of her, and she looked up at me, her blue eyes so clear, unsuspecting, and innocent.

Suddenly I couldn't stand. My legs just collapsed, and I ended up kneeling in front of her.

She said my name. A question. A single syllable that seemed to hold so much. Surprise, confusion, fear.

How could I tell her? How could I be the one to break this news? But also, how could I let someone else do it? Someone who didn't... care for her.

I don't remember exactly what I said. But I remember her eyes seeming to darken. The confusion in them. Her eyebrows furrowing. That perfect mouth asking questions I couldn't answer.

Why would the groundskeeper say such an awful thing?

And could it really be true? Although there have been reports of druidic prophecy, the last I heard, they were still unsure if it's real or just the usual thing of people trying to get fame and fortune.

Tears spilled from those beautiful eyes. I found myself holding Adriana as her whole body heaved with sobs.

I don't know how long we were like that. But suddenly Ms. Hoxha and the librarian were there, and they were pulling Adriana from my arms. I tried to hold on, I really did, but they tore her away from me, saying that her parents were on their way and she was needed in the principal's office.

I tried to follow, but another teacher stopped me. I don't even remember who it was.

Adriana looked back at me as they led her away. She looked so scared. I tried to run to her one last time, but the teacher was faster and held me there while Ms. Hoxha pulled Adriana along by the arm.

I think she understood. At least, I hope that's what that look meant.

School was dismissed early, and we were all sent home.

Mike came by to check I was OK and return my stuff. I had completely forgotten that I'd left it with him.

I told him I was fine, not to worry. That it was obviously some psychosis or something and the groundskeeper was wrong.

He agreed. Of course, he did. It must be wrong.

There's no such thing as prophecy, right? And even if there was, there's no reason for Adriana to die. She doesn't deserve that. She's the purest, most beautiful person in the world. She has to be OK.

So why can't I convince myself of that? And why won't she answer or return my calls?

5 JULY

Adriana is dead.

6 JULY

I don't know how to write this. How to start.

I've heard you should start writing and see where it goes. Which is what I'm doing right now. But I have no idea where this could go.

This makes no sense. This journal, life, everything. No sense at all.

What's the point?

6 JULY ... AGAIN

I'm trying this again. Dad keeps saying I should. Well, he would prefer I talk to him or the school counsellor, but he said I should at least write in this.

So did Leigh. They keep calling and messaging to check on me, wanting to talk. But there's nothing to talk about.

Adriana is dead. That's just the reality.

I'm trying to write here. I really am. I just don't know what to write. It's too awful.

I'm going to try to start from the beginning. From after the groundskeeper said that Adriana would die. Had a prophecy that she would.

It took ages to get to sleep that night. I kept seeing the groundskeeper hunched over the mower, the knife in his left hand covered in blood. Staring at the lizard that had been alive just moments before.

When I finally slept, I had the most awful dreams. I kept running to Adriana. Running and running, searching for her, but it was like trying to run in water, and I was always too slow.

It was in the middle of one of these dreams that I was woken by the house phone ringing. A phone call at 4 a.m. is never going to be good news. The best possibility is an overseas telemarketer.

I wish it had been a telemarketer.

I didn't answer the phone. Pretended to be asleep. Who has a landline these days, anyway? I've been telling Dad for years that we don't need it, that it's old-fashioned and we never get calls on it.

He always says it's "in case of emergency".

I don't know if this phone call counts. The emergency had already happened hours ago.

It was Ms. Hoxha. Calling to say that Adriana had been found dead. That she'd seen me with her the day before and wanted me to know before it hit the news.

Of course, I didn't know this immediately. I pretended to be asleep while Dad answered the phone. But then he came into my room and said my name.

There was something in his voice. A flatness, like he'd pulled down a barrier in front of any emotion in case it came spilling out and overwhelmed him.

That's when I knew something was very wrong.

I pretended to wake up, even though I'd been wide awake since the phone rang.

He sat down on my bed and put an arm around me. Then he said he had something to tell me, "something awful".

I remember getting another flash of the groundskeeper and that gruesome ritual with the lizard. The blood shining in the midday sun. But no, it couldn't be.

Except it was.

Even when he said, "Adriana is dead," I couldn't believe him. It couldn't be true.

He held me.

I don't know how long I cried. It felt like hours, but the sun wasn't yet up when I found there were no more tears. At least not then. There have been many more since.

Then Dad went to make me a warm drink and pancakes for breakfast. I didn't even know he knew how to make pancakes.

It was nice of him, but I didn't taste them. Forcing them down my throat was tough, like they were cardboard. But Dad kept watching me, as if taking the next bite meant I was still alive, so I finished the plate.

Then I excused myself, saying I was exhausted and needed to go back to bed. The sun was only just rising. But somehow what I had meant as a way to be alone ended up being true, and I fell asleep. The next thing I knew, the sun was high in the sky.

I had five missed calls and three messages from Mike, and two missed calls from Leigh. I sent them each a message saying I was OK but needed time. It was a lie, but a lie they needed to hear.

Then I stupidly checked the local news, out of some sense of morbid curiosity. And not just the reputable site but the one that makes money off scandal and gruesome detail.

And the details were gruesome.

The exact words in one news story were "torn to shreds". As if Adriana were nothing but a piece of cloth. They even had photos in her window, showing the edge of what looked like a pool of blood.

The police chief was quoted as saying that the crime looked like a werewolf attack, but it wasn't on a full moon, so they were "exploring other avenues of inquiry".

It couldn't be a werewolf, right? I mean, Dad is a werewolf. I don't even want to think that he's capable of that.

Maybe he's right to not want me to see him on a full moon.

I didn't go to school yesterday, obviously, but it was cancelled anyway. That's how Mike had found out about Adriana and why he'd been calling.

I feel awful about that. I should have called and told him. They used to be close friends too. But I just didn't think of it at the time.

I've been an awful friend lately.

Mike keeps messaging me. Asking if I'm OK, checking if he can do anything. I feel bad that I'm not responding with anything more than the basics.

I want to help him. To support him. But I don't know how. I don't know how to even understand what happened, let alone be supportive.

I feel so empty inside, like I have nothing to give anyone.

I guess now he might finally believe he's not an Asura. He knows he would never hurt Adriana, demon or not.

Why would anyone do that to Adriana? To the sweetest, most beautiful and helpful and wonderful person I have ever met?

The school forum is full of posts with theories, but for once I just don't want to read them. No matter what they say, there is no reason. There can't be.

I don't remember much else from yesterday. I know Dad came up with some salad for lunch, and I made myself eat it. And we watched a movie while having takeout for dinner last night. But it's like something I saw through some dirty glass rather than stuff I did.

School went back today, but Dad said I could stay home. He wants me to go tomorrow, though.

To be honest, I'm scared. How can I go to school knowing that Adriana will never be there again? That, just when she finally found a way to truly shine, her light was extinguished?

And yes, I know that's cheesy, but I don't care right now.

I don't know how I'm going to do it. It was difficult enough right after the change. Those first few weeks when we didn't know what was going on and everyone was scared. The panic and looting and violence. But, even then, I didn't feel like I was really in danger from those who changed.

I mean, it had to have been a critter, right? What else could do that to a person?

The police still have the groundskeeper in custody, but there are no reports of a druid being able to do anything like that. The only thing they've got on him is that he predicted it would happen.

The local druid's guild put out a statement calling it unfair imprisonment. They said something about how a flight of birds had told the groundskeeper that death was nearby, then making the sacrifice told him who.

Journalists keep asking how that works, but all the guild is saying is that they "just know". As if they'd tell us their secrets. Who knows what they can do? Or what some of the other critters can really do?

I want it to be the groundskeeper. To believe he killed Adriana. To hate him and want to kill him back.

But I saw his eyes after he had the prophecy. He was terrified. He wouldn't be a groundskeeper if he was that good an actor.

Why would anyone want to kill Adriana? She is was the sweetest person on the planet. She didn't even let being a muse turn her into the type of person we used to complain about. She just stayed her beautiful, shy, wonderful self. The kind of person no one has ever said a bad word about.

Well. Not no one.

Daisy said some things over the last few weeks. Tried to suggest Adriana wasn't so pure, that she was "giving favours" to teachers for her good grades.

I'd put it down to jealousy, which is typical for Daisy. Adriana had taken over her position as the most popular girl in school, even if she didn't want it. But then Tanya mentioned it on a school forum about Adriana dying, which got me thinking.

Well, it got me writing some angry stuff first, but then I deleted that and thought about it.

It couldn't be Daisy, right? I mean, she's a vampire and all, but why would she do... that... to Adriana's body? Why wouldn't she just drink her blood? According to the news reports and that photo on the tabloid site, there was a LOT of blood.

I messaged Tanya privately and said that, but she said that it would be the perfect way to disguise her guilt. "No one would suspect a vampire with that much blood left around."

Is Daisy smart enough to think of that? And could she have overcome her hunger enough to leave all that food lying around?

I keep trying to convince myself that she's not, could not. But I'm not so sure.

And it's just too much of a coincidence to have this on top of all the other weird stuff happening, right? Weird even for these times. Daisy couldn't have killed Mr. Dane or given Mr. Rusico smallpox, right? Even if she could have, why would she?

I asked Tanya that. She said that Mr. Dane had given Daisy a B– on a pop quiz, which brought her grade down to a B overall and she needed to keep it an A for her dad to keep giving her privileges to go out on school nights. And Daisy had been tipped to play the lead in "All's Well That Ends Well", which Mr. Rusico canned.

But still, she is a vampire, and Mr. Dane died during the day. Maybe she could have given him a heart attack from lack of blood from feeding the night before (is that even how it works?), but the coroner would have found that. And there's no link to smallpox.

I need to stop thinking about this. I know I do. It's the cops' job to find out who killed Adriana, not mine. But I can't help it.

I couldn't help Adriana in life when I should have. Maybe figuring out who killed her will make me feel a bit less awful.

7 JULY

Dad made me go to school today.

It was awful. Everyone kept talking about Adriana. About what happened to her. Some people have really twisted minds and made up stories even worse than what actually happened, which I didn't think was possible this morning.

And the word got around that I heard the groundskeeper and ran to her, so before school even started, people kept coming up to me asking me about it, wanting to know how I "felt" about it.

How am I supposed to feel anything about it?

I didn't have an answer to that by the time I was called to Ms. Hoxha's office not long before lunch.

I wracked my brain while she lit some new incense. She must have gotten some dud matches because they kept breaking on her.

I mean, who even uses matches anymore? If you're lighting stuff that often, why not get a lighter? Maybe she's one of those types who thinks "natural" necessarily means better, even though snake bites are natural and antivenom is made in a lab.

Ms. Hoxha has no plants or crystals around the office, though, so she's not the typical new age type. But she does have that long wavy hair you see in all the commercials for that stuff. And her chair is always covered in scraps of brightly printed wool to the point that you couldn't see any of the cushions or frame. At least it wasn't crocheted, I guess.

Anyway, when she finally lit the incense and sat down, she asked that dreaded question.

"How do you feel?"

At least the head tilt was minimal this time. I can't stand that head tilt.

I tried to be honest. Told her I didn't know. Numb, maybe. Tired, definitely. Sick of being asked how I felt.

She didn't get angry at that last bit. Maybe she isn't as bad as I make her out to be. But she did keep trying to figure out how I felt.

She asked if I blamed the groundskeeper. Turns out his name is Fred. Because of course it is something boring like that.

I honestly said I don't blame him.

I want to, because he'd be someone to blame, but I can't. Not really.

He just had the premonition. He wasn't the one who did it. Or, at least, the cops didn't find his fingerprints anywhere, and he did have an alibi.

I wonder why he's still in custody, then?

Ms. Hoxha said he'd been an investment banker before the change. That would have been rough for a druid, being stuck in an office, using a computer all day. No wonder he quit and became a groundskeeper, though the pay change must have been tough.

I don't know why she told me that. I mean, investment bankers are awful and ruin the economy for everyone else, but that doesn't make him a killer.

Then she asked how I felt about whoever had done it.

I didn't know the words to describe it. To explain the tightness in my stomach, the black clenching ball of pain. The feeling in the back of my throat, almost halfway between growling and that sensation you get when you're about to throw up. The way my vision seemed to become more concentrated, losing all the stuff at the edges.

I guess Ms. Hoxha finally found what makes me angry.

But there's no one to direct that anger to. The cops have no idea who could have done it. And no matter how many rumours and conspiracy theories go around, none explain what happened.

How was Adriana, so beautiful, incredible, sensitive, and sweet, murdered in her bedroom? How was her body desecrated without a scream or any other sound to alert the elf bodyguard just outside her door, even with their enhanced senses? How did the murderer get in through her locked window, or in a door and through the house, again without alerting the elf? And how did they escape without leaving any mark, not even a drop of the blood that must have been all over them?

I tried to tell her how I felt. But I found I couldn't. It was like it was locked behind a door, hiding from anyone else. It's only when I'm alone that I can fully feel it. Then it comes over me, and I get overwhelmed and don't know how to cope with another moment feeling this way.

But somehow I do. I survive each moment, and then the next.

It felt like I was in Ms. Hoxha's office for hours, but I was back on my way to class when the lunch bell rang, so it must have only been about half an hour.

It was a beautiful day, but Mike and I stayed in the cafeteria instead of going to the oval.

I'm so lucky Mike understands. I didn't need to say anything. He just got his food and went straight to an empty table, which was easy since most people were outside.

I finally asked how he was going. I should have asked days ago.

He's coping, but barely. He and Adriana had been friends for a long time. They'd never been quite as close as Adriana and me, but she had been there for him for years while he was figuring out who he was. That meant a lot to him.

Mike said he wouldn't be who he is today without Adriana.

A part of me thought that sounded cheesy. The rest of me just wanted to hug Mike. I decided on the second option.

I don't care what people in the cafeteria thought about us hugging. He needed it. And I did too.

I tried not to cry and failed. So did Mike.

Adriana deserves our tears. She deserves our grief. And we'll give them to her, until we can find the happiness she should have had.

Yes, we're doing poetry in English class. I think Mrs. Liu would be impressed.

I'm supposed to write a piece of poetry for an assignment. A part of me wants to write about Adriana. I might even get some extra sympathy points.

The rest feels like that's not fair to her. That I would be using her death to get a good grade. I don't know what to do.

I think she'd tell me to write it. She'd want me to do whatever was right to get the grades. But maybe I just wish she'd say that.

Did I really know her? Who she really was, even after a couple of years of no contact? I think I did. I hope I did.

Her funeral is on Saturday. Dad made sure my formal occasion outfit still fitted me.

As if Adriana would care. She hated all the old-fashioned stuff her parents made her wear. She'd be happier if I wore a bright t-shirt and jeans. But the Pereira's probably wouldn't let me into their church in that. And I want to be there.

Maybe I could wear something bright and weird underneath, where others can't see it.

Thankfully Mike will be there too. I don't know if I could do it without him.

One more school day. Then the funeral.

I can survive this, right?

Right?

8 JULY

Potential cut short

Freckled skin;

A shy grin.

A fire inside;

A proper facade.

Blue eyes shrouded, enthralling;

Knee-high socks always falling.

A blush that travels from hairline down;

A simple kiss leading to crackdown.

A heart filed with love, but with fear to bestow;

A heart caged by parents and fear of below.

May the soul rest forever in bliss I can't believe;

May I always remember her and one day not grieve.

9 JULY

Leigh came back again this weekend. I feel bad because I know they've got their life and classes and stuff, but I'm also glad they're here.

They're the first person who hasn't asked how I'm feeling. When they came in, they knew not to hug me. Not until Dad was done fussing and was off doing some housework, and we'd gone up to my room.

When they did hug me, it was a really long and tight hug, and I just… broke. I had thought I was all out of tears, but there were more. Ones that seemed deeper somehow, like I'd only cried out the surface tears, and these were waiting beneath, needing to be sobbed out.

I hope I didn't ruin Leigh's shirt with the snot. It got pretty gross, but they didn't complain.

When I was all out of tears again, they just put on some music and we laid down on my bed and listened for ages without talking.

I don't know how Leigh knows how to do just the right thing. They have said we are much alike, so maybe it's just what they would like if they were in my situation.

I like the idea that I'm like Leigh. For an older sibling, they're pretty cool. They don't pretend to be more important or knowledgeable about stuff (even if they are) just because they're three years older than me. They don't treat me like a kid like Dad does.

I know he tries, but he's a parent. I swear, something changes in people the moment they have kids. They become instantly older and more superior somehow. They claim it's because they want to "protect" us, but I think they're just protecting themselves and how they want things to be.

So yeah… then there was the funeral.

I've never been to one before. Or, at least, not one that I remember. My mother died when I was young and I've never asked if I was at the funeral. And when my grandfather died, it was so far away and we couldn't get there in time. He was Muslim and got buried as quickly as possible.

Instead, we observed the *hidaad*, even though we're not religious. It was a long three days. I mean, I'd only met Granddad a few times, and it was school holidays! But Dad insisted it was respectful to refrain from enjoyment for three days. I tried. I really did. But I might have played some online games with Mike on day three.

Because Adriana's parents are Pentecostal, this was a big affair. There was this musical piece to start with. Some teenage guys I don't know on guitars and singing stuff about praising God.

I didn't understand what they were going on about. I don't know much about religion, but it seemed very different from the Christian stuff I'd seen in the movies. At least there was no Latin.

Then all the priests and family came through in this big procession, all walking slowly. Adriana's mother was crying, which made me cry, but her dad was all stony-faced and stoic like always. God forbid (irony intended) that he ever shows emotion.

Then there were hymns and more songs and speeches that painted Adriana as being this angelic person and totally didn't get who she really was. I mean, she was incredible, but not in the way they were saying. The person they saw had no desire but to please her parents and church, with no free will or fire in her soul (if a soul exists). That wasn't the Adriana I knew.

Sitting through the speeches was awful. The collar on my shirt felt too tight around my neck even when I opened the top button. And I was overheating from the suit jacket.

Why do people insist on wearing suits? They make no sense.

Adriana's uncle gave a eulogy. She didn't even like the guy. He always told Adriana that she shouldn't do "boy" things like playing with trucks if she ever wanted a good husband, and gave her frilly dresses and makeup kits for presents. So gross.

The pastor kept saying that Adriana would be reunited with God. I'm not sure if I want that to be true or not. I mean, I don't believe in it, but I do want Adriana to be somewhere she can be happy. Where she can embrace all that she is was.

It felt like the funeral took forever, but it was less than an hour.

Then we all made our way outside for the lowering of the coffin into the earth. The parade of people walking past, saying things that sounded lovely but meant nothing.

When it was my turn, I couldn't think of anything to say that was worthy of Adriana. I just stared at the coffin, which was already covered by a mix of flowers and dirt, and tried not to cry.

I failed.

The church's women's group put on a potluck lunch. Because of course it's the women's obligation to put on the food. I could almost feel Leigh's rage beside me at the gendering and inequality.

At least there was a good potato bake. It even had little bits of crispy bacon in it. Leigh might be vegan, but I can't bring myself to be. Bacon and cheese are just too good.

I found Mike there, and he felt about as awkward as I did. His eyes were all puffy, so I think he'd been crying too. I hugged him but made sure it didn't last too long so neither of us cried more. That would have just made it all worse.

Thankfully, Dad said we could go after I'd eaten. But he insisted we at least "give our condolences" to Adriana's parents.

That was rough. I know they've hated me ever since the day they caught me kissing Adriana. They think I was corrupting their "innocent little girl". I swear her mother glared at me while I was saying I was sorry for her loss, and her father just gave this curt nod. Neither said a word.

And then we just came home. Dad tried to make conversation in the car, but I wasn't in the mood. And I think Leigh gave him "a look" from their place in the front seat. So thankfully I got to just be alone for a bit. And when we got home, I said I needed a nap.

I did try to. But whenever I closed my eyes, I saw that coffin. Stark lines and black paint, so glossy you could see reflections in it until the dirt began hiding it from view.

It wasn't the right coffin for Adriana. But is there such a thing as a "right coffin" for anyone?

So here I am, writing instead of sleeping.

I think I'm finally starting to understand the point of this journalling thing. I want to be able to tell someone this stuff. How I feel. I don't know why I can't just say this to someone, but I can't.

Maybe Leigh is right about the patriarchy making everything stupid and suppressing our humanity.

I don't know. All I know is that life isn't fair. Adriana should still be alive and off becoming a muse, not in some hole in the ground. And that whoever did this to her should pay.

11 JULY

Mike and I are going to find out who did it. We're going to avenge Adriana.

He came over after school today, and we finally talked about how we feel and how it's unfair. How whoever did it needs to be stopped. Who knew where they would stop if they could do something as awful as killing Adriana?

So, we're going to find out who it is.

The police are doing nothing! They finally released the groundskeeper yesterday, after holding him for a whole week even though there was no evidence that he was the one who did it, just that he predicted it. And they admitted on the news that they don't have any suspects.

If they aren't going to do their jobs, we will. This isn't a big town and there aren't many people who would have any reason to hurt Adriana. Let alone be able to avoid her bodyguard and not make a sound while doing it.

Sure, it could be random. But if true crime shows have taught me anything, it's that the more vicious the crime, the more likely it was someone they knew. Because people are awful.

We drew up a list of people it could be.

The first on the list was the bodyguard. Elves seem to have issues relating to most people, to the point that some people say they seem almost sociopathic. But if the Chapter of Muses sent him, he would have been well-vetted. They're harder to breach than intelligence agencies! And elves don't have any extra strength or claws or anything that could do what was done to Adriana. So, we ruled him out.

I argued for her parents, given how much they restricted her, but Mike made some good points. They were going to be set with her becoming a muse, and their God would punish them for something like that. And if nothing else, they wouldn't do it that way: they would want a pretty corpse for an open casket funeral.

Those things are creepy, looking at a corpse.

Then we came back to Daisy. I made all the points about how a vampire wouldn't kill that way, but Mike pointed out the same thing Tanya said: maybe she would want it to look that way so people don't suspect her. He made a good point about how the way Adriana died sounds like something from the types of shows Daisy loves to watch and talk about constantly.

Then there is Tanya or her mother. They're so anti-Creatures that we couldn't put anything past them. And with Adriana's newfound fame, she'd be a perfect target for a hate crime like that, which would explain the violence. But not how they avoided the bodyguard.

Also, I don't think Tanya has that in her; she just believes what her mother says. But maybe her mother is that twisted? And she's certainly not the only anti-Creature type in town.

Mike suggested the goth kids at school because he'd seen them talking to Adriana a few times, but I don't think it's likely. Sure, they like dark music and makeup, but adults made up the association with evil and stuff, Leigh says.

None of the teachers had any reason to be angry at Adriana. She was getting good grades and bringing prestige to the school for having a muse there. And none of the art kids would ever hurt a muse, so that rules out Ayan.

As does him just being him. He talks a big game, but I can't see him being able to hurt a mouse. Maybe a mosquito?

Mike asked whether any of the jocks might have reason to dislike Adriana. I suggested Paul Azeri, because he'd been hitting on her. But there's no way her parents would have let her date, even if she had wanted to, and why would she want to date a jock anyway?

Maybe he got angry when she said no? Even as I suggested it, I know it was stupid. Paul could date half the school if he wanted to, and he seems easy going.

It seemed so fruitless. Adriana didn't hang out with anyone to give us leads. She spent most lunchtimes in the library after we stopped hanging out.

So that leaves the librarian or the other nerds and outcasts who hung out there.

We decided that Daisy is the most likely one, but we'd scope out Tanya's mother and the library nerds too. So tomorrow we're going to hang out in the library at lunch, and I will try to talk to Tanya. She's more likely to speak with me than Mike, because her mother is also racist.

Why do some people get so filled with hate toward all different types of people who've never hurt them? Leigh said it's because they're insecure and want someone to dislike to make them feel better about themselves, but that makes no sense to me. If you're insecure about yourself, why would hurting others make you feel better?

It feels good to have a plan. I'm trying not to think about what we'll do if we find out who did it. Or even worse, if we can't figure it out.

We have to. For Adriana.

12 JULY

Today was a bust. And I feel like I need a mental shower after hearing all the awful stuff Tanya was spewing.

We had PE together. I usually hate PE, but at least there was lots of time to talk while we waited for our turn to hit a ball with a stick.

I asked Tanya what her mother thought of Adriana being killed so soon after being discovered to be a muse. Supposedly her mother had said, "Serves the uppity girl right."

It took a lot of self-control not to hit something. I wanted to be at the front of the line in PE for the first time.

Tanya looked a bit guilty as she said it, which helped. She seemed really awkward about it. Wouldn't meet my eye, and her foot dug into the ground so much she was dislodging soil.

Maybe she's realising her mother isn't a nice person. That's got to be tough.

But I didn't let that sway me! I kept going, asking Tanya if she thought any of her mother's anti-Creature friends could have been the ones to do this.

I swear, Tanya looked horrified. Like she'd never even considered such a thing. Did she truly not realise what that sort of discrimination can lead to? Wasn't she paying attention in history class last year, to the stories of genocide based on race, or the witch trials to destroy women? I mean, anti-critter hatred is basically the same thing, right?

I guess I should stop saying "critter". They prefer "Creature" – anti-Creature hatred.

Tanya swore that her mother and her friends wouldn't do something like that. That they couldn't. That they were all talk, no action. That her mother gets squeamish at even the smallest drop of blood, let alone…

Then she got called up to hit the ball with the stick. I've never seen her run toward a PE task like that, and she sat as far away from me as possible after she was done with her turn.

I want to believe her. But what's the alternative? That one of my schoolmates did this?

On that, spending lunch in the library revealed nothing more than that it's full of nerds who don't speak to each other, and just sit there with their homework or a book.

I don't mean "nerds" in a mean way, of course: I'm a nerd too, in my own way. It's not a bad thing. Just a thing.

But I don't think any of them seemed like the type to even talk to Adriana, let alone be so worked up about something they'd do… that… to her.

But someone did it. And whoever it is will pay.

13 JULY

I spoke to Mike tonight. He said it wasn't the goth kids.

Supposedly they were trying to get Adriana to help them out, to get her to inspire some crappy poetry or music or something. Even though she hadn't had training, they thought just being near her might help.

Based on some of the awful lyrics Mike quoted, it sounds like they needed her help!

> I sit in darkness waiting to see;
>
> The future that lies in front of me.
>
> The dark abyss yawns and draws me in;
>
> A deeper life, waiting to begin.

Stereotypical, much?

Oh, that reminds me. I got a B+ on my poetry assignment. I'm OK with that, but I expected more. Didn't Ms. Lui notice that each couplet was two syllables longer than the one before? I thought that was good!

Anyway, Mike is sure it's not the goth kids. And I don't think it's Tanya or her mother.

So that leaves Daisy.

Of course it would be her. The wealthiest person at school, who probably has loads of security at home. And is a vampire who could easily kill us.

At least that would explain why the cops said there was no forensic evidence at the scene. Her father must have paid them off.

Which reminds me: a kid from the year below me on the school forums tried to say that it could have been a vampire because they can turn into bats, and that's how the killer would have gotten into Adriana's second-floor bedroom without waking anyone.

It's so stupid! Don't they know that the whole "turning into a bat" thing was made up by Bram Stoker? Like, it's less than 150 years old, while vampires have been in myths for thousands of years. Sure, bats were associated with vampires before that, but vampires didn't turn into them.

I don't even know why Bram Stoker's book got so famous. I mean, he wasn't known as any great author before Dracula. And it wouldn't fly (pun intended) today, with how much he messed up Romanian mythology and was super racist and homophobic. Like, it's literally about English people being scared that other cultures might try to invade them, while they were off invading half the world and destroying heaps of indigenous cultures!

Huh. I can tell I've been hanging out with Leigh a lot lately. I think it's a good influence, though.

Anyway, back to Daisy. We need to find any evidence it was her.

Based on all the cop shows I've seen, the first step is going to the crime scene.

Adriana's bedroom.

Where she was…

I'm not sure I can do it. I want to. I know this is how we find any leads the cops missed. But…

I told Mike how I felt about it. Or, maybe "told" isn't the right word. I tried, but I couldn't. Thankfully, he figured out what I wasn't saying.

He said he'd do it.

I feel a bit bad about Mike going through that instead of me. But no matter how much I want to find out who killed Adriana, there are some things I just can't do, and I need to accept that that's OK. I have a boundary.

I hope Mike isn't pushing past his boundaries to do this. But I have to trust that he's telling me the truth when he says he can do it.

So yeah, he's going to find a way to get into Adriana's bedroom and have a look around. See if there's anything that gives us a clue.

In the meantime, I offered to come up with how we would check out Daisy's place.

We probably can't do it until the weekend. We need a time when she's asleep or out of the house, and Daisy's sleep schedule is a mess on weekdays, as she constantly reminds EVERYONE, because she has to be awake for school. But on weekends she sleeps all day, supposedly, so we could go in then.

The next problem is that her mother is a valkyrie. I like how the politically correct way of describing them is "emotionally heightened", when what they really mean is "they can turn on you in a heartbeat, changing from caring to murderous".

Supposedly it's a cortisol regulation issue in the brain, the same thing that happens when you're super stressed. A bunch of scientists are looking into it, testing out medication used for this disorder where you have too much cortisol.

To which Creature rights activists are saying that they don't need a "cure", that we need to make "reasonable adjustments" so valkyrie can live among us peacefully. Well, that and fashion designers need to adjust clothing for their massive wings.

But yeah, we need to make sure we don't disturb Daisy's mother. Valkyrie are fierce and can somehow decide the fate of a battle, so that is not a great idea.

Then Daisy's father is an elf. They're one of those families where everyone turned – the joys of random selection. At least, it's random as far as anyone can figure out so far, though there are LOTS of conspiracy theories about who changed and who didn't.

So with the enhanced senses of the elf, we can't go in while he's there. He'd alert his wife, who'd warn Daisy, and we'd be screwed.

And, of course, there's probably a security system or something, given they're one of the richest families in town.

Maybe going to Adriana's room would have been easier?

No.

I made the right choice.

I guess I should start researching then. Maybe start by looking up their place online.

14 JULY

It's amazing what you can find online!

I did a unit last year on finding reliable online sources, and it has paid off. When the librarian, who was teaching the course, kept going on about being careful about what you post and stuff, I thought they were overreacting, but yeah, there's a lot!

First, it turns out that Daisy's parents are going to the fanciest restaurant in town (which doesn't say much, given this town) on Saturday night for their anniversary, so Daisy is planning to sneak out and head to the park with some friends and a bottle of whiskey she says is really expensive, that she stole from her parents' alcohol cabinet.

I know this because she posted about it on social media. I mean, that's just stupid! Not only because her parents could find out, but she'll probably get a bunch of people there that she won't want.

Anyway, that means the house will be empty. They don't even have a maid at the moment because the last one put

Daisy's mother's stuff away in the wrong place and was lucky to get out of there alive, according to their online job review.

They've been advertising for a replacement for weeks, but the ad is still up and was updated with an increased salary a couple of days ago, so they mustn't have found anyone. Word spreads quickly in towns like this, and there have been a few news reports of valkyrie "accidentally" killing people who annoy them.

I heard the other day that there's even a new legal defence for it. Supposedly it's modelled after the "temporary insanity" defence because they claim valkyrie can't control their rages, so they shouldn't get punished.

I don't know how I feel about that. I mean, it's true, as far as we can tell. They can't control it. Even a tiny annoyance can fill them with blind rage for a minute, and then they become fine again.

But at the same time, people have been killed. Shouldn't something be done about that? Not prison, of course, because that's inhumane (for lack of a better term, given they're not human).

The anti-Creature types use each news story about a valkyrie hurting people to call for them and other "dangerous" Creatures to be kept in "facilities" for their own good.

I don't know why the news stations give those people airtime to spout such stuff. Haven't they learnt any history? Putting groups of people into separate camps generally isn't a sign of a healthy society.

Anyway, back to Daisy! The Nguyen-Smiths bought their house only a few months ago, after her mother got this huge promotion and they wanted to show it off. So I found the listing on the local real estate site, with floorplans and everything! Comparing the photos to the walls in the background from Daisy's video stream at school, I figured out which room is hers.

It's a converted pool house out the back. A "teenager retreat" according to the real estate ad. It even has a games room and a kitchenette.

Must be nice to have your own place, separate from your parents. But then again, if it makes you into a snob like Daisy, maybe I don't want it so much.

The best part is that the security system looks to only be in the main building. There was a 3D video thing and the pool house had no security panels or anything like the ones inside each door into the main house. I guess they aren't too scared, given Daisy could take care of almost anything that broke in.

We'd still probably need to break a window or something to get into Daisy's room, but that's easier than disarming a security system. They always make hacking or short-circuiting security look so easy in the movies, but I doubt we could do that.

Anyway, next I was thinking about how to get in without being seen. That's where the maps website came in. I went into street view and had a look around. The whole property is bordered with this tall hedge, and it's at the end of a cul-de-sac with these massive metal gates that are obviously designed to be intimidating. But the house next door has a short back fence and backs onto a walking track, so we could hop over that, through the hedge and be right on the corner of the property where Daisy's "retreat" is.

It feels weird being all sneaky like this. I mean, I'm planning how to break into someone's place. But it's for good reasons, so it's OK, right?

I don't know anymore.

You know, I was so caught up in figuring all of this out, I haven't stopped to think about it. About what I'm doing and why. About Adriana.

Damn it. I swore I wasn't going to cry anymore. At least not until I'd found her killer and avenged her.

And now I sound like some idiot from a romance novel. That's not me. I just… I miss her.

We'd barely spoken since her parents made us stop being friends, but even seeing her around school was enough. Knowing she was there.

I keep expecting to see her still. When I go into the cafeteria, I still look for her. For that perfect ponytail. I still wait to see her at school assemblies.

And I keep wondering if there was anything more I could have done. Should I have fought harder to stay with her that day in the library? Would it have made any difference?

I don't know. What I do know is that I am going to search Daisy's place on Saturday night and find out if she's the one who did this. And if she is, she's going to pay.

Meanwhile, Mike tried to have a look at Adriana's place today but found it swarming with suits. There were black sedans outside with the logo for the local Chapter of Muses. No doubt trying to figure out if this was a targeted muse thing, more than any care for Adriana as a person.

He's going to try tomorrow.

I'll continue looking into Daisy.

16 JULY

I know this will sound all melodramatic and stuff, but I am writing this in case I don't come back. In case what Mike and I do tonight goes all wrong and something happens to me.

Mike tried another two times to get into Adriana's place, but there was security around the house both times. And on the second time, he overheard one of the suits saying that they'd finished the "sweep and clean", so there wouldn't be anything left to find.

That means we're left with only one option: Daisy.

Dad: know that I love you, and I didn't find you as annoying as I made you out to be. You're actually a good father.

Leigh: you are the most awesome person I have ever met. Everyone says that older siblings are awful and mean and stuff, but you never were. I always wanted to grow up to be just like you.

Mike: if you survived, you were the best friend I could ever hope for, and I'm sorry I dragged you into this.

I guess that's all I have to write. Know that I did it because it's right.

17 JULY

Should I tear out that last page? I mean, it's super embarrassing now, but I hate damaging books. It feels so wrong. I mean, books are great, right? Even ones in physical form. And even just my journal.

But if there's a ripped-out page, wouldn't that draw even more attention to it?

Anyway, obviously we survived. But how long Daisy will last, we now need to decide.

It was her.

We found her journal. She wrote pages and pages about how much she hated Adriana. Called her some of the most awful names I've ever heard, and even some things I don't know and don't want to look up.

It was… graphic. Lots of talk of drinking her blood. Making her suffer. Plans for sneaking into her home to terrorise her.

In one entry, she said, "I want to rip her into ribbons no wider than the ones in her adorable little ponytail."

She actually wrote that. And then she did it.

She didn't write about that part in her journal. She stopped writing the day Adriana died.

I hope she couldn't bring herself to admit what she did, even in her journal. I hope she lives every moment in guilt and shame and all the other awful emotions that eat you up inside.

Or maybe she doesn't have emotions. Only someone truly heartless could do what she did. Could do that to such a beautiful person.

Only someone evil.

So now Mike and I need to decide what to do. He said we shouldn't talk about it yet. He wants to give us time to "ground ourselves" before we "do anything rash". He sounds like my father.

I mean, yes, I was angry. I almost tore the journal in two because I was so tense. But I think I have the right to be a bit furious when I find out my classmate killed one of my best friends!

But no, Mike wants to wait. Why, so Daisy could do it to someone else?

I thought about doing it alone. Going back in last night after Daisy got home. But her parents would be there too. I would still do it. I'd probably die, but I'd still do it.

Maybe that's why Mike insisted on staying the night at mine. Before even asking me, he told Dad he wanted to spend time with me because he wasn't coping well after what happened to Adriana.

Dad seemed to know something wasn't right, but maybe that was because it was a late decision. We didn't get home until after dinner time. He kept looking at us when he called Mike's father to check if it was OK. Thankfully Mike's dad thought it was a good idea for him.

Actually, I'm not sure if I am thankful for it. Mike being there was the only thing that stopped me from going back there. I could have had it done last night. Finished it.

But I can't change that now. Now we must plan our next move.

Mike thinks we should call the police. I think we should stake her.

He seemed shocked when I said that. Then he asked if that's what Adriana would have wanted.

I wanted to hit Mike at that moment.

I think it's stupid how people try to solve things by hitting people. It never solves stuff, just makes it more complicated.

But, at that moment, when he tried to use her name to stop me from taking out her murderer…

I'm not proud of how I felt. I've never wanted to hit anyone before all this happened, and now twice in one week.

I think Mike saw what I was thinking because he had this scared look. Scared of me. Of his best friend. He even took a step back.

Thankfully, that stopped me. I held back. And we talked. We came to a compromise of confronting her. But I told him I'll bring a stake, and I'm not scared to use it.

Now I just need to find the right time to do it.

20 JULY

Seeing Daisy at school has been horrible. Knowing what she's done but being unable to do anything about it. Not yet, at least.

Dad's gotten so protective. He keeps wanting to know where I am and what I'm doing. He'd never let me out at night to confront Daisy. And if he found out I skipped any school, he'd get even worse. So we need to wait until the weekend.

At least she shouldn't know we're coming. We were so careful not to leave a trace, to put everything back where it was. We didn't even have to break the window because she left it open. I know it's a small town and all, but after two deaths and smallpox, I would think people would be more careful than that.

Then again, she wasn't careful enough to hide her partying from her parents. They found out and grounded her, which is good for us.

And her parents are going to a charity gala a few towns over on Saturday night, so she should be home alone.

My stake is nearly ready. I've been going into the woodshop during lunchbreaks I don't have with Mike. Just one more session and it should be good and sharp.

23 JULY

We're about to head to Daisy's place. Based on her usual weekend social media schedule, she should be asleep until at least 8 p.m., but her parents should leave before six for the gala.

That should be plenty of time.

One way or another, this ends tonight.

23 JULY . . . AGAIN

It didn't end tonight.

I'm so frustrated. I wanted this to be over so much. But it has just gotten even more complicated!

So, everything went to plan to start with. Mike and I went out, telling our parents we were going for a walk and hanging out. Then we went over to Daisy's place, snuck in through the neighbour's place and the side hedge and found the window unlocked, just like last time.

That's when things stopped going to plan.

It turns out that Daisy's parents were serious about the curfew. They hired a babysitter to make sure she wouldn't sneak out. And to make it worse, the babysitter was Mauve, who graduated last year.

Daisy used to tease Mauve about her lisp. I can't even begin to imagine how furious Daisy must have been having her be hired as a babysitter, though I'm enjoying trying.

Thankfully we heard Mauve before we were too close. She was talking to herself about how she deserved the jewellery she was taking as payback for everything Daisy had done to her.

I sort of agree. I mean, I generally think stealing is wrong, but it's not like she'll get anything back from Daisy any other way. That would require her admitting she was wrong about anything, and Daisy MUST be perfect.

Anyway, we heard Mauve just as we'd tumbled in through the window and into the bathtub, which was a bit freaky. Oh, and did I mention she turned into a valkyrie? Yeah, another one. Probably hired through a valkyrie club Daisy's mother is in, because all the Creatures have stupid clubs.

So, that wasn't great.

At least she isn't a Creature with enhanced senses. Just one that could have killed us in a furious rage if she'd found us there.

Anyway, we froze when we heard Mauve. The bathroom was next to the bedroom, with the games room and kitchenette making up the other side of the pool house.

We didn't dare talk to decide what to do, in case we alerted Mauve that we were there. We messaged each other instead.

Of course, we'd put our phones on silent before going in. I mean, we're not stupid. It's always a poorly timed phone call that ruins the sneaky plans in the movies. I mean, who even calls these days, other than parents?

Actually, I don't want to go down that train of thought.

Anyway, Mike wanted to leave, to come back another day.

I didn't. I was there for a reason, and I wasn't going to wait any longer to get justice for what happened to Adriana. Even if that meant finding a way to deal with Mauve as well as Daisy.

That's when I realised that Mauve and I essentially wanted the same thing. To make Daisy pay for her crimes. We had been thinking of it all wrong. Mauve would probably be on our side. She'd believe Daisy was capable of killing Adriana and might even help us.

You know, I wonder how many villains in the movies are just the same as the heroes but from a different point of view?

Ugh, I'm getting side-tracked.

I tried convincing Mike that we should bring Mauve into our plans, but he was against it. Thought she'd give us away.

I don't think she would have, but he made a good point. The more people knew we were there if things went wrong, the more risk to us. And Mauve wasn't known for having much of a backbone, which is probably why Daisy felt she could terrorise her.

We decided instead to find a way to get her out of the house long enough for us to do what we needed.

I'm not proud of what we did. But something needed to happen.

We ordered pizza, payment on delivery, under Mauve's name.

Waiting for that pizza seemed to take hours, even though the pizza place has a "delivery in thirty minutes or next one free" rule.

During that time, Mauve must have finished rifling through Daisy's things because she moved to the games room and put something on TV. It was loud enough that Mike and I felt comfortable moving into Daisy's bedroom. We'd need to be quick once the pizza arrived, so we prepared.

Mike did a double-take when I pulled the stake from my backpack. I knew he wouldn't be comfortable with it, but I'd told him I was bringing one. Did he think I'd forgotten? Or that I hadn't been serious?

He'd had the weirdest look, a mix of scared and sad and pleading. I wavered for a moment, but then I thought of Adriana. Of how her eyes crinkled when she smiled. How they glinted when she let go of the facade her parents forced on her for just a moment.

By the time the pizza arrived, Mike had gotten his phone out to record Daisy's confession, and I had the stake ready. I'd taken some deep breaths so my hands didn't shake.

OK, so I did still jump when the phone rang. Again, why do people still have landlines? But we'd put the Nguyen-Smith's number from the online phone book into the order form, so the delivery person must have called when no one answered the front door.

Mauve was understandably confused. She kept swearing it wasn't hers, she'd never ordered it. But she eventually left to talk to the delivery driver in person.

As soon as the door slammed shut, I pulled the lid off the coffin.

(I forgot to write this down the other day, but the rumours were right! Down to the bright pink satin lining, although she'd chosen a more tasteful black brocade outside without the rhinestones I'd heard about. It was even placed on top of her bed – with a matching comforter – which makes no sense.)

Before Daisy opened her eyes, I had the stake above her heart, a mallet in my other hand. She'd looked terrified. Eyes so wide, it was like something from an anime.

I wavered again for a moment, but I wasn't going to let Daisy get away with killing Adriana. Which is what I told her.

It had felt like I was in an action movie.

Until Daisy started crying. Bawling, even. I ended up pulling the stake away a bit because her chest was moving so much.

I had not expected that.

And she was blabbering. Something about how she didn't mean it, not really, she'd just thought it, just written it, but it wasn't true, she wouldn't ever do it, she'd only told that to "her" and wasn't it "supposed to be confidential?"

So yeah, that was confusing.

Mike pointed out that Daisy wasn't going to be able to say anything coherent by the time Mauve got back, so I should put the stake away and help her calm down.

That was tough. I mean, what if it was all an act? Daisy had been cast in that play, right? And she was a vampire. The moment we turned our backs, she could've attacked us.

But Mike was right. We wouldn't find out the truth this way, and we had to go before Mauve returned.

I told Daisy that we needed to talk. That she needed to tell us everything or we'd tell the police. Her eyes got all wide again, after they'd just started to get back to normal, and she agreed to a video call tomorrow.

To be safe, Mike pulled open the blackout curtains while I kept the stake above Daisy's chest. There was just enough sunlight left to be effective, and Daisy could close it after we were gone.

As we ran back to the bathroom and jumped through the window into the sun, I kept thinking that surely she was going to attack us. I could almost feel her teeth in my neck. But all I heard was continued crying.

At that moment, I pitied her.

So yeah, my thoughts are all jumbled. Nothing makes sense.

Who is this "her" she was referring to? And she admitted to thinking about doing what happened to Adriana. I didn't have the heart to say it to Mike, but maybe he's right about the whole Asura thing? But Daisy is a vampire, not an Asura. You can't be both, right?

Yes, I live in a world where I must question whether it's possible to be two mythological creatures simultaneously. If you'd told me that a year ago, I would have laughed and suggested you see a therapist.

We didn't say anything on the way home. Mike wouldn't meet my eyes, which was hard, but he probably needs some time. And we'll find out the truth tomorrow.

Or, at least, I hope so. I hope I can trust Daisy not to betray us. But I don't think I'll be sleeping much tonight. And I'll have the stake under my pillow.

Too bad that "can't enter people's places without their permission" thing isn't true.

24 JULY

I feel like I'm in one of those murder mystery TV shows my grandmother used to watch. Like, the ones she had on DVD because they were so old that they weren't on any streaming services.

You know how in those, you realise the clues were there all along, but you just didn't put it together? And you feel a bit stupid for not seeing it?

I feel a lot stupid.

But at the same time, how could I have known?

I'm going to try not to get ahead of myself and just write down what happened. Maybe if I do that, it will make more sense.

Though, to be honest, writing this in here now feels wrong. But I've gotten used to using this journal to work through what's happening. I'll need to find a way to hide this and make sure NO ONE can read it. Something more secure than under my mattress, which is where I'm hiding it now.

So, Daisy was true to her word. She didn't try to kill Mike or me in the night, and she was even early to our online meeting.

She looked like she hadn't slept in a week. Like, even more dead and gaunt than usual, and that's saying something about a vampire. I think she was trembling.

With a shaky voice, she started talking about how upset she'd been with Adriana for becoming so popular and eclipsing her. How she'd raised it in her monthly counselling session.

Ms. Hoxha had told her to write out her anger so she could let it go. To write down every awful thought to get it out of her head. And Daisy had.

That's why she had detailed how she wanted Adriana to die. "But I only thought it," Daisy kept saying.

While she was talking about that, Mike had been really quiet. His face had been still and emotionless, which only happens when he's feeling overwhelmed by something.

Less than two months ago, it was Mike saying that same sort of thing.

We told Daisy about Mike writing in his journal. How it had come true, and he had thought he was an Asura. But Daisy had another theory.

You know, I always thought Daisy was a bit stupid. That she must have bribed teachers into getting good grades. But today, she actually seemed smart through the fear.

She didn't put on that annoying singsong voice, make any snide comments, or refer to a single influencer or designer. It was like she was a different person.

Anyway, Daisy pointed out that this was the third major issue at our school alone. If Asura were real, this would be happening worldwide, not just to us. And the likelihood of three students at the same school being Asura was just too much for a Creature that hadn't yet been identified anywhere else.

Mike looked as confused as I was about there being "three" of them. But Daisy had put something together that we hadn't. That we should have.

The smallpox, and Ayan's little performance in the cafeteria in the day beforehand.

"A pox on him," Ayan had said. A line from *All's Well that Ends Well*.

It had obviously been intended toward Mr. Rusico. And then the guy got smallpox.

I used words then that Dad probably wouldn't be happy to know that I'd learnt from Leigh. Mike looked a bit surprised, but Daisy joined in.

It was weird. I softened toward her a bit then, which felt strange after being certain one of us was going to kill the other a few days ago.

So yeah, there were three times when someone had said or written something wishing harm on another person and it had suddenly come true: Mr. Dane, Mr. Rusico, and Adriana.

But what was the link? The first and last had been in a journal, but Ayan had spoken his line.

"Hoxha," Mike said in this deep voice I'd never heard from him before. Daisy nodded.

Mike must have seen that I was confused, so he reminded me that Ms. Hoxha had been in the cafeteria that day.

"And she read my journal just before Mr. Dane died," he continued.

"And mine before Adriana, after convincing me it was 'healthy' to write those things," Daisy said. And yes, she did the air quotes and all.

It did not compute.

I mean, Ms. Hoxha was behind it? The school counsellor?

But the more I thought about it, it all made an awful amount of sense. What better cover for someone evil who wants ideas for how to hurt people?

But how could she make Mr. Dane's heart stop beating in the middle of a class? Or give Mr. Rusico smallpox, which was supposed to be extinct? And get past the elf bodyguard to do those awful things to Adriana?

None of us had answers to that. There is no known Creature that has anything like those abilities. Or, at least, I've been keeping up on the latest Creature discoveries since the change, and I haven't heard of any.

So, now we're entering investigation mode. Keeping an eye on Ms. Hoxha and trying to figure out how she could have done this. What she is.

A tiny part of me still wants to believe Daisy killed Adriana. That way, I could just stake her, and this would all be over. I could feel that I had avenged Adriana, and maybe I'd be able to sleep without nightmares. Or have a day when I don't cry.

But I can't deny the evidence. Something is happening that's bigger than Adriana. And it would disrespect her to ignore that just to make myself feel better.

25 JULY

Investigation results: day one

- None of us saw Ms. Hoxha at school today, even though we tried. Does she know we're on to her?
- We've realised that we never see her around town either. It's a small town, so we always see people we know out shopping and stuff, but only Mike had seen her outside of school, and that had been just the once, at the local farmer's market.
- We've pooled what we knew about her:
  - She started at the school after everything changed.
  - She instigated the school journal program.
  - She has terrible taste in incense.
  - She doesn't seem to get as cold as other people.

It's not much to go on yet.

26 JULY

Investigation results: day two

Mike and I watched Ms. Hoxha in the cafeteria today, getting her lunch. She was really quick about it. Went straight from the door nearest the kitchen, grabbed her food, and left.

The only interesting thing was that she brought her own ceramic plate, bamboo cutlery, and plastic tongs. It seemed a weird mix. Why have recyclable cutlery if you've got regular plates and tongs? And why didn't she trust the cafeteria trays or tongs if she ate food from there?

Oh, actually, there was another interesting thing: what Ms. Hoxha got for lunch. She made a salad without dressing or seasoning, before grabbing some fruit. She moved so quickly, it must have been a standard meal for her.

And it was a vegan jambalaya day, one of the few things the cafeteria does well.

I'm not sure that means anything, though. Maybe she's just on a diet? Ugh, why is this so hard?

27 JULY

Investigation results: day three

Ms. Hoxha must spend less time around the students than most other staff at the school because none of us saw her today. But Daisy spoke with some of her friends and got a few more details.

It seems that people will tell you anything if you're popular and they want to be friends with you, even stuff about their counselling sessions.

Ayan said Ms. Hoxha never schedules any of the werewolves into a session around the full moon. There are rumours in the school werewolf club that maybe she's Creaturist, specifically against werewolves.

I don't know. To me, not dealing with teenage werewolves when they're at their most animalistic just sounds like a good survival trait. I'm always super careful around them for the days immediately around the full moon.

Tanya also told Daisy that she'd heard that Ms. Hoxha lives in a cave in the woods, where she makes her incense out of native herbs and spices. That would explain why they're so smoky and always smell awful. But this is from Tanya, so grain of salt and all.

Oh, I discovered the origin of that saying the other day! It turns out that Pliny the Elder guy was involved again. Something about an antidote to a poison that included walnuts, figs, a plant called rue, plus "a grain of salt". So yeah, it seems fitting that it means something doubtful since it comes from Pliny. I still don't know how people follow him.

Anyway, back to the investigation. Anna, who spoke to Daisy AFTER refusing to talk with me(!), said that Ms. Hoxha doesn't have a car spot at the school which was weird because she lives in a beach house (which is like an hour walk away). Anna knew that because she volunteers in the school admin office for extra credit. Anna told Daisy that Ms. Hoxha spends her weekends swimming so much that Anna thinks she might be a selkie.

Yeah, I'm not sure if I believe any of them.

I did get a chance to talk to Megan, though. She's still. . . different. More reserved. She hasn't gotten back into any of her activism work. She even started wearing gloves to Chemistry and hasn't raised the Bunsen burner issue again, which makes me really sad.

Anyway, when I asked her about Ms. Hoxha, Megan seemed confused. Said there was nothing weirder about her than any other counsellor other than the fact that she might be on the autism spectrum. When I asked why she thought that, Megan mentioned some stuff about how Ms. Hoxha seems uncomfortable around big crowds and how she once shrieked like a banshee when some loud feedback came in over the PA during a session. Megan said she thought it was something called "hyperacusis".

I looked it up. It's essentially increased sensitivity to sound. Interesting.

Mike spoke to Mrs. Liu, who is a friend of his dryad dad. It turns out that teachers gossip A LOT. And they try to tell US it's not OK!!

Mrs. Liu said that Ms. Hoxha basically never goes to the staff room or any social functions with the other school staff. They think she's all aloof and thinks she's better than them because she came from a city, unlike most teachers who grew up here.

They supposedly joke about how she brings her own plate and cutlery to the cafeteria and never even touches the tongs to serve her lunch, in case our small town infects her.

Supposedly she once went to a faculty holiday party at the beer garden down at the pub. There was a thing about giving anonymous gifts, and someone gave Ms. Hoxha one of those salt crystal lights. It makes sense; people who use a lot of incense often love those things, thinking they have magical healing properties. But according to Mrs. Liu, Ms. Hoxha had looked disgusted, dropped it immediately and refused to clean it up after it shattered into pieces.

Let's just say that it did not make her popular with the other teachers, and she had left the party shortly afterward.

But even with all that, there's nothing to suggest that Ms. Hoxha could somehow be capable of everything that has happened.

It can't be a coincidence, though. Right? I mean, twice is a coincidence, three times is a pattern. But how?

28 JULY

Investigation results: day four

Daisy and I went to Mike's place tonight to assemble everything we know..

I am still not comfortable around Daisy, even with her helping us. I mean, she could easily kill us. It would take only moments, with vampire speed and strength. And even if she didn't kill Adriana, she still thought and wrote those awful things about her.

I took the stake with me, hidden under my hoodie, but Daisy was on her best behaviour. She honestly seems to be wanting to help. I never expected her to do something so... nice? It feels wrong.

We plotted out everything we know or have been told about Ms. Hoxha. It's a weird list:

- school counsellor
- not from here
- seems to make awful things come true if people say or write it
- copes with cold well

- loves incense
- doesn't like salt candles
- screams at loud noises
- hates crowds
- doesn't interact well with other teachers
- dislikes werewolves
- uses her own cutlery and plate
- eats a basic salad and fruit, nothing else
- lives in a cave or a beach house.

Yeah, none of that matches ANY of the critters on the forums I'm on. And yes, I know, I wrote "critters", because she's obviously evil and nothing like my dad or other Creatures. Right?

We spent hours discussing it, doing searches and trying to figure it out, but nothing. So we're all going to research on our own and see what we come up with. Going to have a video chat tomorrow morning and see what we've come up with.

Onto the forums I go!

29 JULY

Investigation results: day five

We have it! Or, at least, we think we do. It looks like Ms. Hoxha is a type of Creature no one knew existed yet. Well, at least, no one here.

Mike's still uncertain. He thinks it's unlikely that we've found a new critter when the world's best scientists have been obsessed with it since the change. But it all fits!

Last night, I went onto my usual forums with the list we'd brought together, and no one had any idea what Ms. Hoxha could be. Some people suggested a trickster of some kind, like the kitsunes from Japan or a leprechaun from Ireland.

Ms. Hoxha is an average height, doesn't have a beard, and doesn't seem to be obsessed with making shoes, so I quickly decided against leprechaun.

Being a fox-like kitsune would explain why she doesn't like wolves, and the legends say they can take human shape. They're also linked to fire, which could be why she loves incense so much. But they usually appear as beautiful women, and I wouldn't call Ms. Hoxha that. I mean, she must be at least thirty! Though if she was a kitsune, she'd have to be at least 100 to be able to shapeshift, so I guess she'd be looking good for her age.

Anyway, kitsunes rarely attack women, and they supposedly always have a glowing gem with them. None of us have ever seen anything like that or heard anything about it, so I'm pretty sure she's not.

To be sure, Mike put some fried tofu on his doorstep last night, because supposedly kitsunes can't resist it, but it was still there this morning. It seems even the stray cats around the place don't like tofu, no matter what Leigh says about how it just needs to be cooked right.

So, I spent as much time this morning as possible between classes doing more research.

There's Coyote, Anansi, and Loki, but they're individuals, not a type of being. It took hours, but I eliminated all the tricksters on Wikipedia.

Oh, and Ms. Lui gave me detention for being late to class because I only had three more tricksters to research at morning tea. I hope Dad doesn't find out about that.

There wasn't much else of value on the forums I use, just lots of people either coming up with silly ideas or saying we're stupid kids and she's just a normal human we don't like because she's a school counsellor. But I knew it was more than that, so I went further afield.

I found an international forum that compares what Creatures show up in different parts of the world. When I posted the description, I got lots of crap, as expected, but one interesting DM.

"You said she constantly burns incense. Are you sure all the smoke is from that?"

And, to be honest, I didn't know. I mean, I rarely see her outside her office. Looking back in this journal, the only other times have been outside on a foggy day and in the cafeteria, which is known for being a bit smoky.

I replied as much, and the person replied: "She's jinn. How did you not figure that out?".

I'd never heard of a jinn before, so I looked it up. It turns out I have heard of it, but by the name "genie".

Except, jinn are NOT what kids' movies promised me! I mean, supposedly there are some nice ones, but the other ones, called ifrits, are awful!

I said as much to the person online, and she just sent back lots of laughing emoji, followed by something in Arabic that Google translate suggested was her calling me a stupid Westerner with no idea of the world or ancient myths.

Maybe she's right. It turns out these jinn are super ancient and have been in folklore since before Islam was a thing. Many people across the Middle East still believe in them, and there are equivalents in Jewish mythology. How have I not heard of this before?

But the more I read, the more familiar it all sounded.

Jinn were supposedly created out of fire and air, and they leave smoke all around them.

The ifrits use wishes people make to cause awful things to happen. You know, like a teenager writing something horrible in their journal, or saying something while upset in the cafeteria.

And they don't like salt, iron, wolves or loud noises.

Things started falling into place. The more I read, the more everything fit.

I told Mike and Daisy over lunch. Neither of them had heard of jinn either, which made me feel a bit better. They both did their own research, and neither could come up with anything that didn't fit.

So, without any other ideas, we're assuming Ms. Hoxha is an ifrit jinn.

Not going to lie, I'm feeling a lot of emotions about that. I'm SO glad we finally have a reason for Adriana's death. And, of course, for Mr. Dane and Mr. Rusico. But that also means that my school counsellor is essentially some ancient fire demon. And that she used Mike and Daisy's offhand wishes, which they didn't really mean, to literally kill people.

I hope Mike doesn't think that makes him responsible for Mr. Dane in any way. He's not! How could he have possibly known?

That means I need to forgive Daisy too, don't I? I mean, she did write those awful things, and it happened because of that. But it's not her fault, any more than Mr. Dane's death was Mike's.

If we're right, it's all Hoxha's fault.

Which brings us to the point of: what do we do about it?

It turns out that finding out how to banish a jinn is maybe even more difficult than identifying one.

There are a bunch of rituals, but they require belief in Allah, and none of us are Muslim, so that wouldn't work. I mean, I'm sure some people in town are Muslim, and there is a mosque in the next town over, but what are we going to do? Walk into a mosque, a group of non-Muslim teens including a vampire, and ask the Imam to banish our jinn school counsellor? That probably wouldn't go down well.

Jinn are essentially the same as shedim from Jewish beliefs, which expands our group of people who might be able to help. But it still means finding a deeply religious person. I don't know anyone like that, apart from Adriana's parents, and although their Pentecostal church believes in lots of stuff I consider strange, I don't think that includes jinn.

Some sources said the only way to avoid a jinn is to live a "pure" life. But pure according to who? Does just living so that you don't actively hurt other people count, or do you have to do certain rituals or believe in something specific?

According to some of the texts, only the prophet Suleiman has the power to control jinn. Supposedly, he (because it's always a "he") gave the jinn tasks to keep them occupied for all eternity, so they didn't even notice when he died. Well, eternity must have ended for Hoxha to be out and about.

I found some videos of rituals to remove a jinn online, but I'm not sure I'd trust an "ancient ritual" someone has posted on YouTube.

I did find one interesting source, the *Tafsir* by Ibn Kathir, who wrote interpretations of the Quran in the 1300s. According to a passage in this book, jinn have these massive egos that only get bigger when people fear them. That explains choosing to be a school counsellor.

Then another website said something similar. Essentially that the way to get rid of ifrit jinn is to make them feel powerless. And there was one source that thought jinn possessed human bodies and claimed you should blow into the person's mouth and tell the jinn to leave.

So, I guess we find a way to trap Hoxha and blow into her mouth? That sounds really weird and sort of dirty, but I'm willing to give most things a try right now! And I'd do many stupid things to avenge Adriana and ensure it doesn't happen again.

We decided we shouldn't do it at school, though. Too many people coming and going. So we are going to try tomorrow at her home.

Which led to the next complication: figuring out where she lives.

It's a small town, so we figured it wouldn't be too hard, even with the rumours of a cave or a beach house.

But I had detention, so I couldn't follow her home, and Daisy couldn't since the sun hadn't set, so Mike did it. I still haven't heard from him, though, and that was hours ago. I hope he's OK. I mean, I'm sure he's fine. Mike can take care of himself. His phone is probably just flat.

Right?

I just need to trust Mike. He knows what he's doing.

Oh, I just remembered that Dad got my grandfather's old Quran. Maybe there's something in there about these ifrits to help? I'll have a read while I wait for Mike.

29 JULY ... AGAIN

Mike never came home and he's not answering his phone!

His dryad dad called my dad to ask if he was here. That was like 10 p.m., when I technically should have been in bed according to Dad, but he didn't even notice when he came up to see if I knew what was happening.

I had to lie to him. To say I had no idea.

But I do. And I know how to find him.

Mike and I both installed this app earlier this year, so we could figure out each other's locations. It was to make life easier when we were catching up and stuff, and we didn't use it much, but I know where he is.

At the graveyard. Where Adriana was buried.

The websites I read today said graveyards are a common place for jinn to live. That and caves. Places of darkness.

Daisy is going to meet me there.

I feel bad for delaying by writing this, but I want there to be some record. Just in case.

Please let Mike be alive. I can't lose him too.

30 JULY ...
VERY EARLY

I can barely believe what happened, and I lived it.

I mean, there have been times I've wondered if I was actually insane and none of this is real. But, if I was insane, would I think that? I don't know.

I hope writing it down here will help make some sense.

So, I met Daisy a block from the cemetery. I felt like I should have been scared, out at night in a graveyard with a vampire, with no one knowing where I was. I mean, that's something from a terrible teen movie, right? The kind where you scream at the TV, telling the human kid to run away.

But I strangely wasn't scared. All I could think about was that we had to save Mike.

Generally, jinn don't seem to hurt people unless a wish is involved, but who knows what Hoxha would do? She's obviously capable of the worst possible things.

So, we crept into the cemetery, moving toward where Mike's phone was located. It was still on, according to the app. I hoped that was a good thing.

There were two of those big mausoleum things in that section of the cemetary. The kind that rich people get to prove to the world that they were super important. Because somehow an expensive, old-fashioned structure means more than doing good things in life.

We approached the one closest to where we entered the cemetery. A plaque outside said it belonged to the town's "founding father". Some guy who came in where "there was previously nothing" and made "a grand settlement". I had to force myself not to scoff at that, both the concept of this place being "grand" and how it conveniently forgot the First Nations peoples that the dude probably massacred for this supposedly empty area of dirt.

Anyway, we snuck up to the mausoleum. The columns weren't wide enough to hide behind, so we crawled the rest of the way. I didn't hear anything inside, but if horror movies have taught me anything, that doesn't mean much.

I looked at Daisy and inclined my head inwards. She nodded, the most serious I've ever seen her, and went in first.

I mean, of course we'd send the vampire in first. I'm just human!

The sound of a chain breaking was so loud that it surely must have echoed throughout the whole town.

I may have jumped, just a bit. I mean, anyone would, right?

After a few seconds, Daisy beckoned me in.

There was nothing inside except a huge granite casket and an altar with what my art teacher would call a "bas-relief" of a bible. At least the windows were pretty: all stained glass but slightly warped from age.

The casket was carved with deep ridges filled with decades of dirt. There were no leaves or anything inside, just a layer of dusty grime, so it must have been a while since anyone had entered the mausoleum. Then again, maybe it had been set up that way so we wouldn't suspect it? That sounds like something an ifrit jinn would do.

Daisy and I stood above the casket and stared at it. I looked up at her, not wanting to say the words. If Hoxha wasn't inside... My stomach had already started to churn.

There was no way I could have moved something that heavy, so Daisy did it.

The stone seemed to scream as the lid slowly moved to the side. Friction, my science teacher from last year would have called it. The sound filled my head and I cringed, my hands covering my ears.

Then it was quiet. I looked inside.

I've seen documentaries showing what's inside old caskets, but it doesn't prepare you.

There was barely anything left but bones, and even those were cracked, with some places having nothing left but dust. In other spots, some skin had survived but had turned this dark brown colour. Over the top of almost everything was this waxy stuff.

There was a stain on the bottom of the casket, like a liquid that had long since dried up.

The smell actually wasn't too awful, but sort of like some bad meat that's been at the back of the freezer for far too long and somehow still smells off despite being frozen.

I made it outside before I threw up. I'm proud of myself for that. But I wish I hadn't had Chiang Mai noodles for dinner.

Daisy was kind enough to wait a few minutes before joining me outside the mausoleum. I guess when you're technically dead and need to drink blood to survive, stuff about death isn't quite as gross anymore.

So, by the time she'd put the lid back on the casket and replaced the chains on the door, I had been able to clean up a bit.

I could still taste the bile, but there hadn't been anything for it. We couldn't have taken a break to get some mouthwash. Mike had still been in danger, and there'd been only one more place to look. I just hoped Hoxha hadn't heard me throw up. Or, you know, the screaming of the stone.

Given all the noise we'd already made, we weren't as cautious about approaching the other mausoleum.

It was a much more modern style, a block of exposed concrete with the only design features being three vertical lines carved into each side of the door, all the way from top to bottom. The door was made of darkly tinted glass in a black metal frame, so we couldn't see inside. Above the door, the name "Georgio" was carved in gold relief.

The Georgio family owned half the stores in town and thought themselves local nobility, with members regularly on the local council, so one of them having a mausoleum tracked. I think I even remember something about the family matriarch dying a few years ago.

Unlike the last one, this mausoleum had a lock in the door, with a sleek black brushed metal doorknob. It didn't survive much longer than the chain, though; vampire strength can easily break many things.

I remember thinking that I should have been scared of that. Of how easily Daisy could break me like a twig. But I sort of felt empowered. She was on my side, and I'd need her against Hoxha if we were going to survive. According to a bunch of sources I read, jinn are stronger and faster than humans.

Daisy opened the door and strode inside as if she wasn't scared, but I noticed her left hand was shaking slightly.

My views on Daisy have changed a lot over the last few days. I've realised that she's spent so much of her life pretending to be someone she isn't because she wanted the attention she got from it. I guess it just came naturally now.

I had felt a need to reassure her, but I hadn't been sure if she'd be OK with that, so I ended up staying silent and following a few steps behind.

The place was spotless. No leaves or dust. And the only thing in the middle of the room was a black marble plinth with gold handles on either side and a gold vase filled with realistic-looking fake lilies.

I looked at Daisy in confusion. Where was the body?

She gave me a look that screamed "ugh, you're such an idiot" and reminded me of her usual self for a moment, then whispered, "cremation".

OK. I guess. But why bother with a mausoleum if you're going to get cremated so your remains are easily held within a jar? Rich people's logic, I guess.

I started looking at the walls. Maybe there was a fake door somewhere? I started by running my hand along each wall, and Daisy quickly followed suit, but there was nothing but smooth polished concrete.

Then I started knocking on each tile, but none sounded any different. And the same happened when we tried each of the floor tiles.

I was sweating by the time we finished. I want to think it was from the exertion of all of that, but if I'm being honest, it was more because we needed to find Mike, and every moment we didn't was a moment he could be being tortured, or worse. Could Hoxha make him wish something awful on us? Or on himself?

And if he wasn't here, where could he be? How could we find him?

My head started ringing and my vision went black at the edges. I was breathing hard. Daisy must have heard (that vampire hearing and all) and came over to where I was crouched on the floor. She put one hand on either side of my face and looked deep into my eyes.

I'd never really noticed how dark her eyes were, how they looked almost black in the dim light.

"Not now," she said. "Break down later, but not now. Now we need your strong face."

She was right. I knew it. I took a few deep breaths as she looked closer at the marble plinth in the middle of the room. After looking at it from all angles, she gripped the gold rings on either side and pulled.

It wasn't just the top of the plinth that lifted, or even the whole plinth. The tiles immediately underneath came up too, with a hiss of a hydraulic lift.

It revealed steep, rough steps descending into the earth, made of compacted dirt and rock. They still showed tool marks. Probably recently made, and nothing like the mausoleum construction.

After a moment of shock, Daisy started down the steps without a word. I had no choice but to follow her.

The stairs went down about two floors deep. Before even going halfway, the air was so dry that I had to fight not to cough. Nothing like the damp tunnels in all the horror shows. Then again, jinn are beings of fire and smoke, so I guess they probably don't like moisture much.

Before we'd gotten to the bottom, I realised we were in a natural cave. The rock edges were aged but still a bit jagged. Probably a volcanic cave, I thought, thinking back to geology last year.

There was only one way to go, but we would have known anyway from the light coming in that direction.

Its warmth flickered softly on the uneven stone walls.

Fire.

I knew we'd been quiet coming down the steps, but I suddenly couldn't stop thinking that Hoxha might have heard us. That she was ready to roast us with her flames.

I'm ashamed to admit I seriously thought about going back. Heading up those stairs and closing the entrance. Going back to safety.

I looked at Daisy and saw the same thoughts on her face. Her eyes were so wide, the fire flickering over a face that seemed paler than usual, even in the warm light.

I'd forgotten until then that fire is one of the things that can kill vampires.

For someone who had only just come to grips with being undead, the idea of suddenly dying must have been even more difficult in a way.

She looked over at me and I tried to be strong.

"Mike," I whispered to her.

She nodded, swallowing.

I'd let her take the lead at every other point, but this time I walked beside her as we approached the curving tunnel toward the fire.

It wasn't long before we heard the crackling of flames. Only a few steps further, voices. They were hard to make out over the noise, but I'd know Mike's voice anywhere after so many years — though it had been hard to adjust when his voice changed and got so much lower.

He was alive! Didn't sound happy, but the tone seemed more snarky than sad. That was a good sign, and I think I grinned.

We crept forward. Or, at least, I did. Vampires have this thing about moving really quietly, so Daisy looked like she was walking normally but made almost no noise, while I had to put each foot down carefully so I didn't break off any of the fragile rock.

Daisy had the nerve to give me a look as if I was doing something stupid! I can't help being a human who makes noises.

But at least she then gave a little smile.

The voices became louder, and I recognised Hoxha's. Even though I'd accepted that she was the one doing all of this, it was still a shock to have it confirmed. I mean, this was my school counsellor!

The smell of smoke was intense. It filled my lungs and I had to resist coughing. Lucky Daisy, not having to breathe unless she needed to speak.

Around another corner, the tunnel suddenly opened into a circular cavern. A lava bubble, if I remember my geology right.

We couldn't see either of them yet, but the cavern was set up like a studio apartment. A black wrought-iron bedframe, with a weird bright blue mattress and no sheets. I guess it must be hard to sleep with soft linens when you're made of flame and smoke.

Beside it was a black wrought-iron and glass bedside table. The glass looked warped, as if it had partially melted then become solid again. Upon the table was a manilla folder and what looked like two standard-issue journals from school.

She must have been looking for more awful wishes to make a reality.

It was then that I realised I'd wanted to be wrong. Wanted my counsellor not to be some malicious genie from ancient

Middle Eastern myth. I mean, is that really too much to ask?

It seems so.

We continued, me taking small steps and Daisy getting annoyed at every little noise I made as we approached the cavern.

One more step and I saw them!

Mike was there, tied up in chains coming from the ceiling made of what looked like moving smoke, but that somehow were solid enough to hold his wrists.

He looked so tired. His eyelids drooped, and it looked like the chains were the only thing keeping him upright, even though his feet were on the ground.

Just writing that made me realise how tired I am. Like, I want to keep writing this, to get it all down. But, at the same time, it's becoming difficult to focus on how to draw the letters.

Is "draw" even the right word? I don't know.

I really need to get some sleep. But then I'll get back to this. I need to write it down while I still remember it all. Before it all seems like just some strange dream.

30 JULY ...
STILL EARLY, BUT
NOT AS EARLY

OK, I got a bit of a sleep. Not much, but I don't think I'll be sleeping well for a while. Not after what happened.

So, I was up to when Daisy and I were standing there, staring at Mike as he was chained up in Hoxha's lair (I think that's a good word for it) below the cemetery.

The guidance counsellor / ifrit sat cross-legged on the ground before a fire set in a fissure in the wall only a few metres from Mike, poring through another journal. Her brow was furrowed, and she threw the journal away, in our direction, with a grunt of annoyance.

I glanced at the book. In big, glittery letters on the top was "Anna". Of course. My cousin might be irritating, but I doubt she's even capable of thinking of an evil thought. Or any original thought.

"Why are all you children so useless these days?" Hoxha roared. And I mean really roared! Like, so loud I could feel the words pulsing through me, vibrating through my chest.

Somehow, though, Mike responded without any fear in his voice, just weariness.

"You mean because we're generally decent human beings who want others to be happy?" The sarcasm was so strong, I couldn't help but grin. I looked at Daisy and saw my smile reflected on her pale face.

Although Hoxha had her back to us, her scoffing noise suggested she didn't appreciate that idea.

"Humans are always full of ill wishes. That is the way of your species!"

Mike laughed. He actually laughed!

I felt some strength returning to me then. Some hope.

"Maybe when we thought the world would provide for us," he said. "But now we know we're screwed, so the best we can do is help each other."

Pride. So. Much. Pride.

Hoxha roared again. A primal sound that was somehow a mix of a burst of flame and a serpent hissing.

It stopped me in my tracks for a moment. My skin crawled as the sound washed over me, making all the hairs stand up.

We were so close. Only ten metres or so away. Mike hadn't seen us yet, which was good. He might've given us away.

But ten metres seemed like a hundred when Hoxha decided to punish Mike for his outburst. She stood and placed one hand on either side of his face. His eyes widened instantly. His breath started coming in short, sharp gulps, and he broke out in a sweat within seconds. A vein in his neck suddenly popped out and pulsed rapidly.

Perhaps the worst part, though, was the smell of burnt flesh, as smoke snaked up from where Hoxha's hands gripped Mike's cheeks.

It only took a few moments for all of this to register, but in those seconds Daisy and I were both struck still. She recovered faster than me, of course.

The first I knew was a blur of movement. Suddenly, Daisy was holding the counsellor down on the cavern floor. This time, the feral roar came from Daisy, as Mike collapsed as much as he could while tied up. Thin tendrils of smoke still trailed off each charred cheek.

I tried to move, to run toward the scene and help, but it felt like I was moving in slow motion. Just like in my dream after Adriana died. No matter how fast I ordered my body to move, it wasn't fast enough. It felt like trying to run in a pool, like the smoky air was actively working against me.

And it was, in a very real way. I could feel my chest tightening and I started to wheeze as the smoke triggered my asthma. But I couldn't let it stop me.

In what felt like several minutes but must have only been seconds as I ran the short distance to where Hoxha and Daisy were wrestling on the ground, the ifrit had showed her true form. Flames spread across the rock, masked by thick black smoke that, rather than lifting up to the ceiling, formed bat-like wings. Her body was so skinny I could see every bone, including those so deformed I didn't want to focus on them. The flesh, if you could call it that, was a mottled orange colour.

Hoxha/the ifrit flared, flames radiating, and Daisy pulled away. I don't blame her for that. She could have died. But at that moment, Hoxha managed to grab Daisy by the throat, a skeletal hand of flame wrapping around that small, pale space. Daisy's eyes widened as she tried to pull back, her arms flailing, but without success. Hoxha pulled closer, and the stench of burnt flesh filled the air again.

Somehow, I found my way to run at normal speed again, almost like the pool of smoke holding me back had swirled away for a moment, and I barged into the jinn. I could feel the heat radiating from the thing starting to burn my face.

It let go of Daisy as it stumbled to the side. I swear it looked surprised as it turned to me, even though its face was mostly fire and smoke.

Those eyes. They were like balls of flame circling in the eye sockets.

I froze as they focused on me. To the side, I could vaguely see Daisy collapsed on her knees, hands at her neck, a look of excruciating pain on her face.

But I couldn't focus on that. Couldn't help Daisy. Or Mike. Not with those awful flaming eyes staring at me. With the jinn slowly approaching, the smoke was getting thicker and thicker. It felt like the smoke was wrapping around me, blocking out the light of the fire. All I could see were the flickering flames that vaguely suggested a humanoid shape, and those terrible, blazing eyes focused on me.

I started coughing. The tickle in my lungs had become a burn. It felt like the heaviest weight at the school gym had been placed on my chest. But even as my lungs and brain screamed in unison for me to move, I stood transfixed.

I tried to fight its power. To think, to move.

I remembered that me being there, scared, was just going to make the ifrit stronger. The way to defeat a jinn was to prove that it was powerless, right?

And yet there I was. Entirely in its power as it moved slowly toward me, taking its time as if it knew I couldn't escape.

At that moment, I had a flashback to a movie Dad had made me and Leigh watch when we were kids. This weird singing and dancing thing that had supposedly been big when he was a kid but seems super problematic now. But there was this line in it, one that stuck with me even though I can barely remember any of the rest of the film. It had felt like what I wanted to say to most of the adults in my life but had never been bold enough to.

And thinking of Leigh and Dad helped. Made me realise that I could do it. Had to do it. It wasn't just Mike, still hanging from chains of smoke, or Daisy, still collapsed on the floor, her chest moving in hacking sobs.

It was everyone. My family. Mike's family. All the teachers and students at my school. Everybody who lived in my town.

I remember thinking that if we didn't stop Hoxha now, no one else knew. Well, except for this journal. And who would believe that after we went missing?

So, despite the flame burning my skin and the smoke filling my lungs, I somehow managed to regain control of my body.

I stepped forward. The jinn looked shocked. The flames in those awful eyes flared brighter and swirled even quicker.

Before it could recover, and before I could lose my nerve, I grabbed hold of the ifrit's jaw.

I could feel my hand burning, but only in a weird, distant way. Like it was happening to another person or was a memory, not something happening to me right then.

Maybe it was the lack of oxygen. No matter how much I tried to breathe, I was only getting little gasps, but I wasn't going to let that stop me.

The ifrit seemed surprised. Hesitant, as if not understanding what I was doing. I barely understood it myself.

With strength I didn't know I had, I moved closer to the thing until I was face-to-face with it. With what little air I had left, I blew that line from the movie into its mouth. "You have no power over me."

It felt like I screamed it, but I doubt it came out as more than a hoarse whisper.

And for a moment, I found I truly believed it. With Mike and Leigh and Dad and even Daisy in my life, something like this couldn't control me. We could stop it.

This thing didn't deserve to exist in our world, no matter how messed up it was.

With everything we'd already been through, with all the times I'd felt I had no control over what was happening, this I could control. I could decide not to let this demon have power over me.

Then, the world around me changed in an instant.

The form of fire and smoke seemed to be sucked into a vortex, like its very existence was being eliminated from reality. Within seconds, it collapsed into a sphere that disappeared with a loud pop that left my ears ringing. In its place, a black and orange snake writhed in agony on the floor, then stopped moving.

I stared at the snake, trying to make sense of it. Its amber scales glowed in the firelight, then fell off as the body dried out to a husk, as if it had been dead for years.

Daisy interrupted my concentration by grabbing the creature and twisting its head off.

"Just to be sure," she said, her voice a bit raw.

I blinked a few times, still confused and barely able to breathe, though at least the smoke was decreasing.

That's when I remembered Mike.

The chains had disappeared, probably the moment the ifrit had, and Mike had collapsed to the ground. His face was burnt and blistered, but he was awake. He was alive.

I ran over and put my arms around him.

I don't know how long we just held each other. I'll let him tell his story if he wants to, but I'll admit I cried. Who wouldn't, after all of that?

While we sat on the ground, just letting each other feel, I watched the snake's corpse dry out more and more until only a skeleton remained. Then Daisy ground it into dust with a boot.

I almost felt bad about that. I mean, people didn't get to choose what they became. What if Ms. Hoxha had been a good person who had been turned into a horrific Creature against her will? Was it right to desecrate what remained of her?

I'll probably never know. If anything, I don't want to. I want to believe that what we did was right.

Eventually, once I could finally breathe properly again, Mike and I got up.

I made the mistake of putting a hand down to help get up, not realising it was the one I'd held the jinn with.

That's when all the pain hit me. Like every moment I'd been able to ignore it came back all at once.

I screamed and collapsed. I think it freaked Mike and Daisy out, but as soon as they saw my hand, Daisy helped me up and started leading the way out.

Thankfully her neck had already started to heal, but Mike's cheeks were blistered and charred. No such super healing for us humans.

Wordlessly, we followed Daisy out of the cavern, up the stairs, into the mausoleum, and stumbled out into the fresh air.

Oh, that air. So sweet and fresh and full of life. The smell of grass and dirt. The chill of it on my seared skin. I breathed deeply, even though it made me cough again.

The first thing Daisy did was throw up. Repeatedly. Then she sat by a planter and sobbed.

I tried to ignore that she'd thrown up blood.

I'd never seen Daisy look so young and naive before. Like a normal, scared teenager who'd had to do awful things, rather than a vampire who could kill me at any moment.

I went to help her, but Mike pulled me back. He was probably right. Daisy wouldn't have wanted my empathy in that moment, and she deserved time to be vulnerable.

A while later, she had pulled herself together and we all stumbled out of the cemetery toward the hospital.

On the way, Mike told us how he'd gotten caught.

He'd hung around the school for a while, pretending to do some homework on his tablet. Knowing Mike, he was probably actually doing homework but didn't want to say that in front of Daisy. No matter how nice she'd been lately, he was still a little wary from years of her teasing.

Anyway, eventually he saw Hoxha leave and followed her. Maybe he hasn't watched enough of those shows about how you always follow way behind and stuff, because he'd only gone a few blocks when he thought she was acting weird, like she knew he was there. He tried to play it cool, to look like he was just pottering along, but Mike will never make an actor. I remember his dryad dad laughing once, before he was a dryad, telling Mike's lumberjack dad that Mike doesn't have an inside face. It took me a while to figure out what that meant.

He'd been passing some shops and decided to duck into one for a moment to pretend that was all he was doing. Except, of course, Mike just entered the first store he came across. Which happened to be a baby store.

The way Mike told the story, he was surrounded by lace and ribbons, not to mention weird pumping devices. Oh, and aisles of pink and blue, plus "gender reveal party" stuff.

He literally shuddered while he was telling us. I think it traumatised him almost more than the whole thing in the cave with Hoxha afterward.

So, he tried to look like he was just browsing for a moment before leaving, but then the storekeeper asked to search his bags. As if Mike would want to steal anything from a place like that!

By the time he got back out, Hoxha was gone. She could have gone down any side street or into a shop. Mike tried to look for her but had no luck, so he decided to go home.

He was going down an alley that was a quicker way home when he was grabbed from behind, and suddenly there was a hand over his mouth and smoke filling his lungs.

The next thing Mike knew, he was in the cavern, tied up with those weird chains of smoke.

Hoxha had… questioned… him. Mike didn't go into detail, but his face said it wasn't good.

Even through all of that, he hadn't told Hoxha about Daisy and me. He'd claimed he'd figured it out all on his own.

I don't know if I would have been that brave if I had been the one caught.

I stopped for a moment as we walked and gave Mike a big hug, before continuing toward the hospital.

I don't want to go into all the fuss that happened there. The doctors and nurses and all their questions. At least they allowed us to stay together because we were all waiting for the healing elf to come by. It seems they were still hanging around after being sent here when Mr. Rusico got smallpox, just in case.

It was the first time I'd ever encountered a healing elf. They seemed annoyed at having to deal with something as mundane as burns. They made this "tut" noise as if we were beneath them, and rolled their eyes when I said they should look at Mike before me.

The police arrived while the elf was just finishing working on Mike and then turned to me, which was lucky because we hadn't discussed a cover story beforehand and my mind went blank. But Mike came up with something about him and Daisy going out to have a bonfire in the woods, and me finding them there, then us getting attacked by a large animal, which we fought off but got burned in the skirmish.

I didn't think Mike was very convincing and I kept waiting for someone to call us out on it while they were taking down their notes and making reports. I'm not sure they were allowed to talk to us without our parents there. Then again, saying that probably would have made things worse for all of us and made the police more likely to investigate and find out we were lying.

I really did hate having to lie, but it's not like we could tell the truth.

'So, yeah, we killed our school counsellor. But it's OK because she was a genie, and not the good kind.'

Yeah, that wouldn't have gone down well. So, we lied, and each added our own parts to the story, until the doctors and police seemed convinced. Or maybe just confident that we wouldn't change the story and hadn't been involved in anything too illegal.

Then Dad came. And Mike's dads and, eventually, Daisy's parents. They all fussed so much, it was embarrassing, but there was something comforting about being embarrassed together.

While Dad was making a fuss, a nurse wrapped up my hand. Although the elf's work had ensured the burns wouldn't get infected, I was warned it would still take a week or so to heal and would be just as painful as usual.

I should be thankful, I guess, but I suspect the elf could have done more if they'd really wanted to.

Not long later, the time came for us to head home. But first, we had the tightest three-person hug I'd ever experienced.

We didn't need words. Enough had been said. We would permanently be bonded by what happened. By what we now knew about each other. Our shared knowledge and pain.

And in a strange way, it felt almost like Adriana was there with us too. A part of that shared bond. At least, I want to think so, even though I don't believe in all that stuff.

I know that's soppy. But I'm too tired to care right now.

And that's how I'm home now. I tried to sleep, but I think it will be a long time coming.

The sky outside my window is starting to lighten. I'm thankful it's for the dawn, not a fire. Although I guess the sun sort of is fire.

Anyway, I think I will watch the sunrise, then try to finally get some sleep. Maybe if I take some of the painkillers the doctors gave me, that will help.

1 AUGUST

I met Mike and Daisy at the cemetery this afternoon, just on dusk. For once, I was thankful for the approaching winter. The sun set early enough for us to meet before the curfew Dad had insisted on, especially after the "animal attack" the other night and how I'd gone out without telling him. And how I'd lied about not knowing where Mike was.

Yeah, I should have thought of that when we came up with the cover story. He seemed so disappointed in me that I wanted to tell him the truth. But if I did, he'd probably think it was another lie to cover up for the first one.

He suggested again this morning that I see a therapist, and I think I might take him up on it this time. At the very least, they couldn't tell anyone else what I tell them, so I can be honest about everything that's happened. Sort of like in this journal, but with someone who can talk back. That actually sounds nice.

Being at school today felt so weird. So wrong. I mean, everyone else was acting like it was normal. Like nothing life-changing had happened.

Well, except for when I overheard someone in the cafeteria at lunch saying they went to their scheduled session with Ms. Hoxha and she never showed.

As far as we can tell, no one knows what happened. There were no police at the school or any questions being asked yet.

The only questions I've gotten are about how I hurt my hand, since it's all bandaged up. Oh, and from teachers asking if I can still do some of my assignments. I mean, I could probably do them since it's not my main hand, so it will be slow typing but not too bad. I'm not going to say that to any teacher, though. Not if they'll give me an extension instead.

At the cemetery, the mausoleum looked just as we left it: the darkened glass door closed and appearing secure, even though the lock was broken.

There was still the stench of vomit outside. I deliberately didn't look at Daisy when I smelt it, given her vampire senses would have detected it long before mine. And it's not like I'm any better; we just hadn't gone past the mausoleum with my puke outside it.

As we walked across the cemetery, we picked up single flowers from random graves until we had a full bouquet to put on Adriana's grave.

It was still so fresh, with only the tiniest shoots of grass pushing up from the dirt.

Those tiny bits of green felt like a lot, though. Like a sign of life, even in the memory of death.

I knelt beside the grave, my knees sinking into the loose dirt.

Mike knelt beside me while Daisy, hooded in a thick cape against the last rays of the sun, stood a few steps away.

Since the funeral, they'd put in a gravestone.

"Adriana Aline Pereira," it read. "Beloved daughter. Now a muse for Jesus Christ."

They'd forgotten to include "adored friend". That was just like Adriana's parents.

On the day of the funeral, I hadn't been able to speak. Today, I finally felt able to say something.

"Adriana," I started, then stopped for a moment. My throat felt sore and I had to clear it.

"I hope you're free now," I continued. The next bit was the hardest to say. "Know that I love you. That I've always loved you."

I don't know if she could hear. I'm generally atheist, so most of me doesn't think she's still around in any form. But a part of me hopes she is. Or that, at the very least, she knew I loved her before she died.

Then I cried. A lot. I hope the tears will help water some new grass.

It was fully dark by the time I could control myself again. I found Mike and Daisy holding me, supporting me as I let it all out.

I expected that from Mike, but I was surprised about Daisy. She's really not as bad as I had thought. I hope she continues to be herself now, rather than that spoiled brat she was pretending to be.

We slowly made our way back to our respective homes. Daisy's place was first. We went the same way we'd snuck in, through the neighbour's place and the hedge. Daisy gave us each a long look at the door to her pool house, then hugged us both. I swear, she nearly broke a rib; vampire strength is not overrated. But any bruising I get is worth it.

Then Mike and I walked back to our part of town in silence, our footsteps in sync as we wandered along the familiar streets.

We stopped outside my place.

It took a while before I could look into his face. When I did, I saw my own emotions echoed there. Grief, sorrow, and the inability to process what had just happened. But also empowerment and achievement.

We hugged for a long time, taking care not to touch each other's burns.

Without another word, Mike left and I went inside.

At least I know I still have one best friend. Who I have no doubt will be a friend for life. And maybe even a new friend in Daisy.

No matter what the universe throws at us.

Dad wasn't home yet, so I went straight to my room to write this.

I think I need to get a new journal. After everything that's happened, it would feel weird to just write about my normal life in this from now on. Whatever "normal" means these days.

But for the first time in a long time, I think I'm finally OK with things being normal for a while. With being just a boring human.

BE KEPT INFORMED

Thank you for reading JUST HUMAN. We hope you enjoyed it.

If you would like to be kept informed of further releases by Angel Hellyer, or other new books from Hague Publishing, why not subscribe to our newsletter at:

www.HaguePublishing.com/subscribe.php

And if you loved the book and have a moment to spare we would really appreciate a short review. Your help in spreading the word is gratefully received.

ABOUT THE AUTHOR

Angel is a queer writer and communication professional.

An avid reader as a young person, Angel loved losing themselves in fantasy novels, as well as roleplaying games. But they didn't consider themselves creative and, following a rough childhood, prioritised clarity in life so they studied maths and computing.

As Angel grew into their authentic self, they realised they actually loved the greys between the blacks and whites. They moved into a communication career, applying creativity professionally and building belief in their imagination.

After a vivid dream in 2013 that they thought would make a great book chapter, Angel wrote (over the course of eight years) their first novel, The Design of Resistance, and eventually self-published it.

Over this time, they became far more progressive than they would ever have expected from their rural Queensland upbringing, working both personally and professionally to advance social justice, equity and equality. So it wasn't that surprising that their second book idea was inspired by some progressive social media posts.

Angel lives in Canberra a chatty and fluffy cat.

Read more about her at:https://angelhellyer.com/about/

'JUST HUMAN' ORIGIN STORY

In 2021, I, like so many other people, found myself in need of something to do with my time. I had recently self-published my first novel (which, like the first pancake, was OK but certainly not the best).

However, I'm not one of those ultra-creative people with all the incredible ideas. I need inspiration to strike, but I can never predict when it will.

Then I stumbled upon two posts on social media in quick succession. The first pointed out that most recent shows and books designed for teens with werewolves and vampires are focused on romance, while young people these days are more about social justice.

The second post was about wanting stories where humans are the ones looking after their supernatural friends instead of them always being the other way around. In particular, part of the post suggested a storyline where humans petitioned the local council to build a wooden climbing frame in the local play-ground instead of the existing iron one, so their fairy friend's children could use it.

I loved this concept. As a person who tries to be as aware and inclusive as possible, it presented an opportunity to explore my passion for social justice through an urban fantasy setting.

And for some reason, a diary-entry style called out to me. I didn't realise until much later that part of my love of the style is that I am not a very visual person. I focus on narrative, on the storylines and connections. Graphic novels are wasted on me, because I find myself jumping from speech bubble to speech bubble!

Thus, *Just Human* was born.

It was an absolute joy to write. I got to research so many myths and legends, and play around with ideas of how worldviews would change in this new reality. I also loved finding places to insert some of the many random facts I know that, for some reason, never come up at trivia nights.

Within eight months, the story poured out of me. And I am so proud of what I was able to create.

I never wrote the story to be published; that has been a delightful addition to the thrill I had writing it! And it is enabling me to share the joy I had writing *Just Human* with others, which is perhaps the most incredible thing a writer can experience.

Angel Hellyer

Hague

Publishing

www.HaguePublishing.com
PO Box 451 Bassendean
Western Australia 6934

www.ingramcontent.com/pod-product-compliance
Lightning Source LLC
Chambersburg PA
CBHW070311190726
48291CB00012B/1076